Best Wishes,

Margaret C. Cooper

# SOLUTION: ESCAPE

## BY MARGARET C. COOPER

*Illustrated by Rod Burke*

WALKER AND COMPANY · NEW YORK, NEW YORK

# For Janice, Larry, and Karen

Library of Congress Cataloging in Publication Data

Cooper, Margaret C.
    Solution: Escape

    SUMMARY: In the 21st century, 13-year-old Stefan
is sent to a scientific research station where his
movements are closely monitored. He discovers he is
a clone, destined to be part of a fanatical scheme to
control the government.
    [1. Science fiction]   I. Burke, Rod.   II. Title.
PZ7.C78736So 1981        [Fic]        80-50496
ISBN 0-8027-6404-5
ISBN 0-8027-6405-3 (lib. bdg.)

First published in the United States of America in 1981 by the Walker Publishing Company, Inc.

Published simultaneously in Canada by Beaverbrooks, Limited, Don Mills, Ontario.

Trade ISBN: 0-8027-6404-5
Reinf. ISBN: 0-8027-6405-3

Library of Congress Catalog Card Number: 80-50496

Book design by Robert Barto

Printed in the United States of America

10   9   8   7   6   5   4   3   2   1

# CHAPTER

STEFAN looked about carefully as he crossed the gravel pathway. No one was in sight. He undid his woven metal belt and eyed it with distaste. 'They must think I'm stupid not to know that there's a homing device in this thing!' he thought. He slipped the belt among the branches of a bush. Feeling free at last, he jogged over to the wide landscaped area that separated two of the main building complexes of the Scientific Research Station at Stovlatz.

A bitter wind, unusual for late June, blew in from the north. Stefan watched grain stalks rippling in the distance as it swept across the great plains. It whistled its way among crumbling border markers, now obsolete since the unification battles of the twenty-first century. And finally reaching the foothills, it gusted strong, molding Stefan's tunic close against his body.

The boy shivered and glanced nervously over his shoulder as he reached the open ground.

Behind him lay the gray dome that housed the nuclear reactor and three concrete laboratory buildings. A low, angular structure built of dark stone held living quarters, a medical wing, and the security section. Even the expanse of cropped grass dotted with square bushes that stretched before him, had a stark, forbidding aspect.

Yet this area had a strange fascination for Stefan. In the month that he had been studying at the Station, he was often drawn to walk alone by the grassy strip that separated the two complexes. The handsome main building of the Public Relations Complex stood in strong contrast to those buildings on Stefan's side. Huge windows ran along its length, and in the front a colonnaded veranda softened the rather narrow entrance.

'I'll never get much closer than this,' Stefan thought, 'not with that bloody Barrier out there.'

He shuddered at the thought of the invisible fence of deadly laser beams. Activated by the presence of body heat, the Barrier prevented unauthorized passage between building complexes.

A flock of crows startled Stefan as they flew overhead and swooped downward. He held his breath until they all landed safely.

Since his arrival four weeks earlier, he had seen two birds dropped in mid flight by those powerful lasers. The instant they had come within range of its heat sensors, the Barrier had snapped into action. The birds plummeted to earth, their bodies drilled neatly through with laser burns.

Up ahead of Stefan a gray-uniformed guard appeared striding towards him. Swiftly the boy knelt and began to search among the grass blades. The guard stopped beside him. "What are you doing here?" he demanded. "This is a restricted area!"

"I'm a student," Stefan answered, "and I'm gathering insect specimens."

The guard pulled Stefan to his feet and read aloud the name tag on his tunic.

"Stefan Yanov. Age 13. Clearance-Research. Student Code Number Cl-1." He looked at Stefan curiously. "Well, you're the first kid I've seen around here. What makes you so special?"

Stefan looked down. "I'm not, really. It's just that Dr. Zorak wants me to find some creatures with exoskeletons for a project we're doing. I'll have them in no time." He knelt down again.

The guard seemed satisfied when he heard Dr. Zorak's name. He shrugged his shoulders and walked off. His huge boots crushed the grass underfoot into a faint path. Stefan, watching out of the corner of his eye, realized at once that the guard's patrol route must run parallel to the Barrier.

He noticed anxiously that two of the crows were now quarreling noisily not two meters beyond the guard's pathway. The larger of the two was pecking greedily at a seed pod. His glossy feathers shone purple in the sun. Each time he lifted his head to swallow, the smaller crow dodged in to steal a few morsels. And each time, the large crow would arch his neck and land a firm peck on the small one's head. Finally the smaller crow changed his tactics. He opened his wings and ran forward swiftly, snatching the treasures from under the very beak of his adversary. Then he launched himself into the air and came swooping over the grass to land near Stefan's feet. The large crow cawed angrily and followed close behind him.

Stefan sat transfixed. He stared at the two birds in disbelief.

"How did you two rascals get through that Barrier alive?" he whispered.

Leaping to his feet, Stefan began retracing the guard's path. As he moved beyond it, a faint rosy glow appeared beside him. He was activating the lasers. When he reached the area that the crows had flown through, he paced back and forth several times. Yes, it was as he'd suspected—rosy glow, then nothing, and then rosy glow again.

Shaking with excitement, he bent down and worked off one of his high boots. It would retain his body heat long enough to be usable as a testing device. Stefan thrust the boot in front of him and swung it from right to left. He noted just where the sparks began to snap against the boot, and where they left off. The air was soon filled with the smell of burning leather, and Stefan's boot was perforated by dozens of tiny, smoldering holes. But he was certain now that there was an opening in the laser fence! The beams broke off for a distance of about four feet wide and five feet high.

Stefan didn't stop to think. He stomped his foot back into the damaged boot, hunched over and eased himself through the open section.

Once on the other side, he drew a deep breath. Darting swiftly from bush to bush, he approached the huge gray buildings he had examined so often from afar. There, he straightened and walked up to the door. He stepped quickly inside and found himself in a dim central hallway.

Ahead of him, a harsh glare of lights illuminated the caretaker's station in the main lobby. Stefan turned abruptly to his right, where a flight of stairs led to the upper floors.

Stefan mounted the steps slowly. A sense of unreality crept over him, raising the hair on his neck. He had never been inside this building before—why, then, did it seem so familiar to him?

# CHAPTER 2

THE doors that lined the narrow halls on the second floor were locked, but Stefan could see that one at the end was slightly ajar. He ducked inside quickly and closed the door behind him. The room was small and airless. Along one wall there was a large rectangular window. The glass was a milky gray, revealing nothing of what lay on the other side of it.

A narrow table and four chairs were arranged in front of the window. Stefan sat in the middle chair and examined the console of instruments set into the surface of the table. He flipped the first switch and a fan in the ceiling began to whir. The small dial directly in front turned smoothly under his fingers, and slowly, like the lifting of a mist, the glass window began to clear.

Stefan found himself staring down into a brightly lit class-room. A black-haired boy about thirteen years old sat alone at a desk. His head was bent over an open book.

Stefan frowned. There was something eerie about the scene. What was it? The curtains were the same as his, the exercise bench was similar, the woven rug identical and—with a start, Stefan's eyes swept back to the boy...

As if he felt Stefan's gaze upon him, the boy looked up.

...Yes! That boy looked exactly like him!

Stefan banged frantically with his fists against the thick glass. "Can you see me?" he shouted. "Here I am, up here! Who are you?"

There was a sudden rush of air behind Stefan and he was grabbed roughly from behind. A muscular arm wrapped around his neck and steel fingers pinned his wrists behind his back.

[6]

Turning his head slightly, Stefan saw that his captor was a uniformed caretaker.

"Let me go!" he shouted. "I want to talk to that boy! Who is that boy?"

The caretaker glanced over Stefan's shoulder into the room below. His eyes widened, and momentarily he relaxed his grip.

Stefan tore away, lunging for the door. Before he could turn the knob, the caretaker's hand sliced forward in a well-aimed karate chop to Stefan's neck.

A muffled roar sounded in Stefan's ears. The walls of the room tipped crazily and the soft-tiled ceiling slid down to enfold him.

# CHAPTER ● ● 3

GRADUALLY Stefan became aware of cold fingers exploring a painful area on the side of his neck. He was lying stretched out on his stomach on a low exercise bench. Opening his eyes carefully to narrow slits, he peered out through a screen of eyelashes. On a nearby table he saw his own electron microscope and racks of slides. He realized that he was back in his own classroom again.

Across the room a door swished open and hurried footsteps came toward him. An angry voice rang out.

"What are you doing to this boy? They tell me he was knocked out by one of your idiot guards—or caretakers, as you call them. Why isn't he receiving medical attention instead of lying in here?"

Stefan knew that voice. It belonged to Professor Lev, his biophysics teacher. He was surprised at the brashness of this usually reserved man.

The cool hands withdrew from Stefan's neck abruptly. Their owner straightened up and stepped forward. Now Stefan could see the tall, narrow form of Dr. Igor Zorak, director of the Research Station.

"I appreciate your concern about the boy, Professor Lev. He is here because I wished to examine him privately before this incident became a matter of official record." There was a sharp edge to the director's silky voice. "I am interested to know if your informant also told you where the boy was found."

"At the moment, that is of little importance. What does concern me is the safety of my pupil. Stefan was brought here to study, not to have his young head knocked off!"

There was a hostile silence. Then Dr. Zorak said coldly, "Perhaps you may think it of some importance when I tell you that he was caught beyond the Barrier—in Environment B—inside the observation cubicle!"

Professor Lev's anger deflated like a popped balloon. His round eyes behind their thick glasses became anxious.

"But that is incredible! Did he get through to the other boy?"

"Not quite. He seems to have caught a glimpse of Cl–2 through the one-way observation glass, but Cl–2 could not have seen him."

Stefan couldn't believe his ears. Dr. Zorak was speaking about him in terms of letters and numbers as if he were referring to a laboratory experiment.

Professor Lev groaned. "You were so certain that this couldn't happen, but they found a way."

"If Cl–2 had not become sick, he would have been far away

by now. I have had them in close proximity before at various times. Until now, everything had gone smoothly."

Professor Lev seemed too involved in his own thoughts to grasp the threat in Dr. Zorak's voice. "Ah, yes," he mused, "but the boys are older now. There may be a strong extrasensory attraction between two minds so much alike. That is a factor over which we have no control."

"Control, my dear Lev," cried Dr. Zorak, "is an issue on which we do not agree. Why was your pupil out on the grounds without his directional belt? You know how carefully we monitor the whereabouts of our people here!"

"Stefan is a bright boy, perhaps brighter than we know. He seems to have become aware rather quickly that there is a directional device in his belt." Professor Lev smiled. "He just took it off when it became inconvenient."

"Such behavior amuses you?" Dr. Zorak's neck flushed dull red. "Yes. It is your indulgent attitude that has made this incident possible!"

Professor Lev, a head shorter than the other man, drew himself to his full height. "Such an incident has always been a possibility. The human mind is ingenious. We must always remember that we are dealing with human beings. A very special kind, I grant you. But they must never be considered less than human."

Suddenly Stefan felt sick. What were they talking about? His head seemed stuffed with cotton and he couldn't make sense out of the words he was hearing. Dr. Zorak's voice pierced his confusion like a steel blade.

"Watch yourself, Lev!" he warned. "How dare you speak to me in this manner? I have been in charge of this experiment for many years, and I don't need advice from you. I find you insubordinate as well as dangerously irresponsible!"

Professor Lev hesitated a moment as if to calm himself. "There are bound to be differences of opinion in a project of this nature, Doctor," he said. "I have become fond of Stefan in the month that he has been my student. But I do not think that has clouded my scientific judgment."

"We shall discuss this again at a later date," snapped Dr. Zorak. "The boy may regain consciousness at any moment. You will please see me in my office tomorrow at 1300 hours." Dr. Zorak strode briskly to the door, where he turned. "When the boy awakens, he will be confused. You must play up that confusion and convince him that his memory has been affected by the caretaker's blow on his head. It will be in your own best interest to succeed at that task, Professor."

With a hiss of compressed air, the door slid closed behind him.

At once Professor Lev bent over Stefan and spoke to him in a low voice. "I have been watching you, Stefan, and I know that you are awake. Trust me. I am your friend. All this I will explain later. For now you must pretend to come to slowly. No matter what I may say to you, don't argue. Just act as if your neck hurts and that you still feel dazed."

Stefan stared fearfully into the eyes of his teacher. "But why should I pretend any longer now that Dr. Zorak has gone away?" he whispered.

"He has not gone. Soon he will be up there, watching." Professor Lev indicated an area behind him with a slight motion of his head.

Stefan's bewildered gaze swept across the familiar back wall of his classroom. The upper half was made up of three solar reflecting mirrors. The middle mirror was larger than either of its mates.

Perspiration broke out on Stefan's forehead. Of course, that was the window of an observation cubicle. And here he, Stefan, was the one being observed!

# CHAPTER

ONCE he was sure that he was alone in his own room, Stefan sat up slowly on his bed. He cradled his aching head between his hands as if it might fall off at any moment.

'Good old Professor Lev,' he thought, 'telling me to *pretend* that I'm dazed and in pain. If those clumsy caretakers had jolted the stretcher one more time on the way up here, I would have passed out again.'

He pulled down his shirt collar and examined his neck in the dresser mirror across from his bed.

"I bet there will be some gigantic bruise there tomorrow," he muttered.

The face he saw reflected in the mirror was pale. The short black hair was rumpled and the gold-flecked amber eyes wide and anxious.

"What's going on around here?" he asked the face. "People hitting me and spying on me through two-way mirrors... MIRRORS!...

Was someone watching him through that very mirror he was looking into now? He leaped from the bed to the dresser. With a frantic heave, he pulled the smooth molded piece of furniture away from the wall. Squeezing in behind it, Stefan examined the back of the piece and then the surface of the wall. It was painted the same gray-green as every other wall in the complex. Stefan sighed with relief when he saw that the rough-textured plastoblocks were unbroken.

'I guess Dr. Zorak is more interested in my academic work than in my personal life... but I'm not taking any chances.'

He began a thorough search of the small rectangular room. Gray light slanted through his narrow, curtainless window in thin disapproving rays.

First Stefan got on his hands and knees and crawled along the floor, tracing all visible electrical wires to their sources. Then he emptied his worktable of his microscope and instruments and felt along the inside panels for any telltale knobs or buttons that might be the microphone of a listening device. He found nothing. His small built-in bookcase and clothes closet were clean, too.

By this time, throbs of pain were traveling down his body all the way to his toes. He lowered himself carefully onto his bed and tried to relax. But his mind kept grinding out questions. None of the experiences he'd had that day made any sense to him. Not the 'hole' in the Barrier, the observation cubicles, nor the boy who looked like him.

"Who can he be?" Stefan cried aloud. "In fact, who am I?"

How strange that he had never really asked that question before. Stefan had known that he was an orphan and therefore a ward of the state. Since he had been a schoolboy it had been drilled into him that he must study hard so that one day he would be able to repay those who had been so generous to him. And he had been told that it was unwise to ask personal questions.

That was after he had left his childhood and the farm far behind. A pang of sadness swept over Stefan as half-remembered smells and bright blurs of color echoed in his mind.

Stefan's only clear memory of his early childhood was of the day it ended. It had been autumn and the afternoon sun shone orange through the maple leaves outside the kitchen door. Inside the ancient stone walls of the farmhouse Stefan was cuddled on the warm lap of his old nurse, Tonia. He could feel her body stiffen when the two strange gentlemen came back into the room and signaled her.

"Stefan, my dear," she had said, "you are five years old now and too big for nurses and for rocking." She lifted him gently off her lap and placed him on the floor. Her clothes had smelled of starch and newly baked bread as she bent over him. "You have done very well on all the tests that these gentlemen have given you. And now it is time for you to go away with them to be properly educated."

"Oh, no, Aunt Tonia," he had answered promptly. "I must stay here and help you and Uncle Peter on the farm."

Tonia had turned her face away from him. Her plump red hand passed over her eyes, but she had said nothing.

Stefan had known then that he stood alone. Tonia was going to let the two strangers take him away. He did not belong on the farm. Hot tears had crowded into his eyes but he squeezed them back—the men were watching.

'And it's still the same today.' Stefan thought, burying his head in the pillow. 'The men are still watching me. I suppose they have always been there, hiding behind special windows, listening to everything I say!'

Stefan checked himself abruptly. This kind of thinking was really crazy—paranoid like one of those cases he had learned about in psychology.

He closed his eyes tightly. Tiny filaments of light swam back and forth across the crimson of his inner eyelids.

'What has happened to my mind these past four weeks that I've been here at the Station? Why do I have such weird dreams about myself—drilling with soldiers, sick in bed with a fever, programming computers, playing soccer? I've done none of these things.'

Stefan rolled over and stared at the ceiling. 'But I was wide awake today when I saw that boy. Is that the next step—that I see myself all over the place even in the daytime? Maybe there are no two-way mirrors or listening devices. Maybe I'm losing my mind!'

Something lurked in the back of Stefan's memory, waiting to be discovered. It had to do with Professor Lev. Concentrating hard, he pulled it out. 'Wait a minute,' he cautioned himself, 'it was Professor Lev himself who pointed out my observation cubicle, and what was that he said to Dr. Zorak about "identical minds" and … and … "the other one"?

'In great excitement, Stefan leaped to his feet and began pacing his room.

'And Zorak said something about "Cl–2" and about being "in charge of this experiment"! They had to be talking about me and that boy I saw. Whatever this mystery is all about, that other boy and I seem to be in it together!'

That thought gave Stefan a strange thrill. Suddenly he didn't feel quite so alone. He undressed and crawled wearily into bed.

'Tomorrow' he promised himself, 'I'm going to have a long talk with Professor Lev. He said that I could trust him!'

STEFAN was awakened the next morning by a brisk knock on his bedroom door. Before he could rise to answer it, a key rattled in the lock and the door opened.

A faint odor of medicine preceded the ample form of the staff physician as she entered.

"Good morning, Stefan," she said. "I hear that you met with an accident yesterday. Now just turn your head to the right and let me examine the injured area for a moment."

Obediently, Stefan twisted his neck to one side. The physician's hands were not gentle. He winced and shrank away from her.

"Hurts, does it?" she asked. "I think you'd better come over to my office where I can take an osteograph."

"Any bruise hurts when you press on it like that," Stefan protested. "I can move my limbs perfectly well, so no bones can be broken."

"I do not recall asking for your medical opinion," the physician said dryly. "Dr. Zorak himself has asked me to examine your injury. Get dressed immediately and I'll see you in my office in ten minutes."

"But I haven't even had breakfast yet," Stefan said as she turned to leave.

The physician dismissed this detail with a wave of her hand and disappeared out of the door.

Grumbling, Stefan eased himself into his tunic. He took the elevator to the main floor and made his way along carpeted corridors to the medical wing.

The physician met him at her office door and ushered him into the examining room.

"Just take off your shirt and stretch out on the examination table," she said as she busied herself at a side table.

Stefan undid the same fastenings he had done up only minutes before. He lay back on the white table. The bright light overhead hurt his eyes.

As the doctor approached him, Stefan could see that she was cradling a long needle along the inside of her wrist.

"Hey!" he cried in alarm. "What's that for? I thought you were just going to take an osteograph!"

"Now, now," she said reproachfully, "this is just a muscle relaxant that will make it easier for us to get a clear picture of your spine."

Out of the corner of his eye, Stefan could see her checking a sterile bottle that hung upside down from a movable frame beside the table. Then the needle bit deep into his skin and found the vein just above his elbow.

The light over Stefan's head glowed even more brightly and then seemed to dim. Voices buzzed in his ears like high-frequency mosquitoes. Then his eyes focused again on the white uniform of the physician.

"We're all finished," she said cheerfully. "The bruise is only superficial and there doesn't seem to be any further damage. It will be uncomfortable, however, for several days."

Stefan sat up slowly. His mouth was dry and his throat felt scratchy. "You're finished?" he asked in astonishment. "But I don't remember anything. Was I unconscious?"

"Not really," she answered lightly, "muscle relaxants often make people rather drowsy. Go back to your room and lie down for an hour. You'll be fine."

Stefan dressed quickly. He noticed that his 'special' belt had reappeared. He buckled it on without comment. He wanted to get away from there as soon as he could.

The physician looked up from her files as he passed her on the way out of the office. "Behave yourself now, young man!" she said.

Out in the corridor, Stefan breathed deeply. He didn't like that doctor. She was so impersonal, as if she viewed him as a specimen rather than a person. In that way, she reminded him of Dr. Zorak.

He stopped at the window and looked out. It was a balmy spring day. The sight of the green grass and linden trees swaying in the breeze refreshed him. He smiled as his stomach growled noisily.

'No wonder I'm hungry,' he thought, glancing at his time-piece, 'it's 1200 already—noontime! I was in that doctor's office for two whole hours. What was happening to me all that time?'

Professor Lev was nowhere to be found. Stefan looked in his office, in the media center, and in the three laboratories. No one on the staff could tell Stefan where he was, nor did they offer to help him find out. Stefan interrupted a group of technicians in the locker room where they were buzzing together about some upcoming official visit. He politely col-lected their lab coats for recycling, but not one of the men offered to pass on any information to him.

At times like this, Stefan wished he was not on an indi-vidualized program. His brief friendships with other boys in the past had been superficial, but at least he'd had someone around to talk to. Here at Stovlatz everyone was too much on edge to pay attention to him.

On his way to the cafeteria, Stefan remembered that Pro-fessor Lev had an appointment at 1300 in Dr. Zorak's office. Well, he would see to it that he caught the Professor on the way back from his conference. With that decision made, Stefan could concentrate on lunch. He would start his meal with black coffee to clear his head, and then have an enormous plankton seafood salad and a serving of chocolate torte. His stomach rumbled at the prospect.

Half an hour later, Stefan stood in the hall outside Dr. Zorak's suite of offices on the main floor. He could hear loud voices coming from the conference room. Stefan hoped that

Professor Lev was standing up to Dr. Zorak.

He shifted impatiently from one foot to the other. He folded his arms and leaned against the door leading to Dr. Zorak's private study. Then on impulse he turned, slid the doors open, and slipped inside. Had the two men in the adjoining room heard him enter?

There was an unnerving silence. Stefan poised himself to run. Then Professor Lev's voice began again, heavy with emotion. Stefan crept closer to the door between the two rooms.

"Oh, I quite understand the situation now, Dr. Zorak," Professor Lev was saying bitterly. "You believe that the possession of that information will guarantee you my full cooperation."

"Quite right," returned Dr. Zorak. "Your talents both as an instructor and nuclear biophysicist are well known. You were chosen to teach Cl–1 here where the laboratories and the reactor are available to you at all times." The older man paused to add weight to his next words. "I on the other hand, am not only the administrative head of this station but the psychiatrist in charge of this project. I have directed its progress for over thirteen years, and I flatter myself that all has gone well—until now! I will take any steps necessary to assure the success of this project."

The floor boards began to squeak and Stefan could picture Professor Lev pacing up and down. When he spoke, his voice sounded defeated.

"I begin to see your point, Dr. Zorak," he said. "Perhaps our differences are not as great as they seem. They are based largely on procedure. These boys have been placed in an artificial environment. They have no family, little security or affection. Yet we hope that they will develop into human beings who..."

With a voice like a clap of thunder, Dr. Zorak interrupted

him. "These boys are *clones*! We already know both their strengths and their weaknesses. Intelligence will be nurtured, but willfulness must be crushed!"

A cold chill ran up Stefan's spine at these words. He was afraid to move; afraid, almost, to breathe.

In the other room, Professor Lev persisted, "But what is in store for these boys in the future? The scientific communities of the world forbade genetic experiments as far back as the year 2000. How will it be possible for them to take government posts and work as a team as you plan? Your clones may be rejected by the people."

The chair creaked as Dr. Zorak rose. "When the time comes, only a few of us, serving as advisors, need even know that they are clones. Or even that there are more than one of them. Surely you know that doubles, stand-ins, look-alikes are used by all the great leaders in the world today."

Professor Lev cleared his throat before he spoke again.

"Then each of these two boys is to become an expert in one of the crucial branches of power. But what of the military, Dr. Zorak. aren't you forgetting the main...?"

Once again Dr. Zorak interrupted him. "I forget nothing! I shall be there to 'guide' these clones in their future career. Then, as now, everything shall be tightly controlled."

"Why do you speak of only one 'career'?" Professor Lev's voice rose in disbelief. "Do you mean these boys to take over a prime leadership position as one man?" The pitch of his voice sank slowly as he answered his own question. "Of course you do. That would avoid the question of clones altogether. And you, Dr. Zorak, will be there in the shadows...the power behind the throne!"

"Many great statesmen have filled that role, Professor Lev. But I can see that our time is up now. Good afternoon."

Professor Lev mumbled something in return, and Stefan heard the door swoosh shut after him. Silently, Stefan slid out

the study door and rounded the nearest corner in the corridor unnoticed. There he fell onto a bench trembling from head to toe.

'Trust me — oh, sure, you can trust me!' he repeated to himself. 'It sounds like that coward Lev is going to work hand in hand with Zorak. I should have known he was no friend of mine.'

In spite of his bitter thoughts, Stefan found himself heading directly for Professor Lev's apartments. 'Let him just try to explain all that... and what in the gyrating universe *is* a clone?'

# C H A P T E R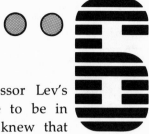

STEFAN pressed urgently on Professor Lev's door buzzer. He had no clearance to be in this part of the building, and he knew that a patrol would soon pass by.

The audio box at his side crackled and Dr. Lev's voice inquired, "Who is there?"

"It's me, Professor Lev—it's Stefan. I've got to talk to you. Please let me in quickly!"

"You may now enter." Professor Lev's voice imprint whirred through the computer and three tumblers in the door lock snapped. The door swung open silently.

Professor Lev hurried towards him. "What are you doing here, my boy? You are supposed to be resting in your room right now."

"Oh, you really keep track of me, don't you? Whose side are you on, anyway? You said I should trust you—but I heard what you and Dr. Zorak were saying about me. You..."

Stefan stopped his head was reeling again. The drowsiness that had been dispelled by the coffee came back.

"Sit down, Stefan, and lower your voice," said Professor Lev sternly. "You must learn to be cautious. I will explain to you what I can."

Stefan remained standing. "Do you think I'd believe one bloody word you said after what I just overheard?"

"Give me two minutes, Stefan. If you aren't convinced that I'm telling the truth, you can yell your foolish head off, and we'll both take the consequences."

Stefan sank down into a nearby chair.

Professor Lev began pacing up and down in front of Stefan. "You must have overheard the conversation between Dr.

**[23]**

Zorak and me. But, Stefan, did you hear the whole conversation?"

"No, I couldn't make out what you were saying at first. But when I got inside the study, I heard Dr. Zorak talking about some experiment that isn't going well."

"Yes. He made that point about halfway through the conversation. Dr. Zorak disapproves of the way I'm treating you. He thinks I'm giving you too much freedom. Your education requires total effort, concentration, and discipline. Dr. Zorak doesn't want that concentration broken in any way, by anyone. Did you hear him bring up the subject of my family?"

"Your family?" repeated Stefan in surprise. "No, why would he do that?"

"It was a threat, Stefan. You see, I came to this Scientific Research Station knowing only that I was to teach a gifted young student in one of the best-equipped facilities in the country. I was delighted to take a leave from the University and come here. I soon found, however, that I was involved in an experiment in which human lives are being manipulated in an unethical fashion. Such a perversion of modern science goes against everything I believe in."

"But why don't you fight Dr. Zorak?" interrupted Stefan. "Why don't you expose his schemes?"

"That is where the threat comes in, Stefan. Dr. Zorak has gotten his hands on some letters I wrote to my brother when I was a young graduate student. In them I was foolish enough to criticize the achievements of our government's space program. I named names as well as missions."

Stefan was puzzled. "But everyone knows that our technical progress has been very slow for several decades."

Professor Lev shook his head. "Oh, no, Stefan. Those of us working in the field know that, but it is far from common knowledge."

"Could those old letters hurt you now?" asked the boy.

"Yes, they could. They would also cast official suspicion on my brother, and my entire family. So you see, Stefan, why Dr. Zorak believes he can command my total cooperation."

"But you've got to help me, Professor Lev. I have no one else I can turn to. Will you at least answer some questions?"

"I'll tell you as much as I know. Unfortunately, it may not be enough to satisfy you."

Stefan didn't waste a moment. "Is that other boy I saw Cl–2? Does that stand for 'clone'? What is a clone?"

Professor Lev smiled wanly. "You believe in getting right to the point. And so will I." He cleared his throat. "As you have gathered, Stefan, you are involved in a highly controversial experiment. You are a clone. A human clone is a perfectly ordinary person in every way except in the manner of conception and sometimes birth. Most humans are the result of the union of a sperm and an egg, which grows to maturity in a female womb. A clone can be grown from an already complete human cell that has been placed in a substitute womb."

This explanation was like the sudden shock of cold water in Stefan's face. His mind became instantly alert. "What do you mean 'already complete' cell? It sounds like something wrapped together in plastic."

"That's not entirely wrong, Stefan. Every cell in an organism carries a full set of genetic information, just as a fertilized egg does. Once the cell has been chemically instructed not to specialize into a specific organ, it can grow like a whole normal egg into a whole normal person. You, for instance, were produced from the skin cell of an adult male. Both you and Cl-2, whose name is Evonn, by the way, are exact replicas.

"Then Evonn is the boy I saw through the observation window! I thought he looked just like me. We're like...identical twins, then?"

"That's right, Stefan. And aside from age, you are also exact replicas of the man from whose skin cells you were grown."

Stefan didn't like the way that sounded. "What are we...a couple of freaks?" he cried. "Are we some kind of private sideshow, Professor Lev?"

"No, no, Stefan. Calm down. If that were the case, you wouldn't be here in a research institute receiving a first class education."

"A research institute! Now I get it. This Evonn and I, we're not just involved in someone's experiment, we *are* someone's experiment, aren't we? Someone who doesn't really care that we are human beings, too... Someone named Dr. Igor Zorak!"

Stefan's face flushed red and his amber eyes sparked in fury. "Why didn't he just clone himself, Professor Lev? He could have had a dozen ugly little Zoraks running around. Why did he have to use us?"

Professor Lev's face creased into lines of sympathy. "It is difficult to comprehend, Stefan, and more difficult to try to explain."

Stefan didn't hear the Professor's quiet voice interrupt him. His sense of outrage grew with each new thought.

"And, and what about the guy who donated his cells—our 'father'? What kind of a person is he, to take part in an experiment like this? Who could be so egotistical that he'd rather have exact copies of himself than have normal children?"

"I'm sorry, Stefan," said Professor Lev, "I don't know the answer to that question. I just found out about Evonn myself, and I know nothing about your clone-father."

Stefan sank back wearily into his chair. "You know, Professor, in a way all this makes sense to me. I've always felt— well, removed from other people. It's like there's something missing in me. Maybe when you're a clone, it takes two of you to add up to a complete person."

Professor Lev strode quickly over to Stefan and held him by both shoulders.

"You *are* a complete person, Stefan! You have spent most of your life moving from one learning center to another. You never had time to form close ties with people. Perhaps you realize now what you have missed. But what you have gained is also important—independence, self-reliance. The fact that you have a clone-brother doesn't make *you* any less of a person. Stefan, listen to me. Don't develop a 'clone-mentality' now!"

Stefan stood up. "I think I'd better go and lie down for awhile. My mind is in a muddle."

"I'm sorry. I know this is a shock to you." Professor Lev patted Stefan's shoulder sympathetically. "And it's no wonder you're tired—Dr. Zorak told me they'd given you a truth drug to find out how you got through the Barrier."

"Oh, of course!" cried Stefan, "I should have known! Well, what did they find out?"

"Very little. Either you had a superhuman hold on your subconscious or you really don't know how it happened. I'm not going to ask you that question."

"Thanks, Professor Lev, but I'll be honest with you. I was as surprised to find that there was a hole in the Barrier as they were to hear about it. But did I say anything about the other boy—Evonn?"

Professor Lev shook his head. "You did say that you'd seen a boy, but nothing more than that. Your neck must have been bothering you, for whenever the questioning progressed to the point where you saw the boy, you got very excited and began babbling about being hit by the caretaker."

Stefan sighed. "Good. Then I didn't give them much information in those two hours."

Professor Lev started and looked at his timepeice.

"Stefan!" he said sharply, "aren't you due at the media center now? You are late—someone will already have checked your room when you didn't show up. There may be a patrol out after you, and you'd better not be caught here."

"Maybe the doctor notified them that I was supposed to rest for awhile. Can you call Personnel and find out what is happening?"

Professor Lev went to the communicator. "Central Personnel, please," he said with authority. "Hello. Professor Lev here. Will you please inform me of the whereabouts of my student, Stefan Yanov. I wish to contact him about an assignment."

There was a moment of silence, then the treble vibrations of a woman's voice reached Stefan across the room.

Professor Lev's answering voice sounded shocked. "You did?" he asked. "He was? Are you quite certain?"

The vibrations increased in volume and then ceased abruptly.

Professor Lev turned to Stefan. "They know exactly where you are, she told me. Your room was just checked, and you are now fast asleep in your bed!"

STEFAN'S heart was pounding so loudly in his ears that he scarcely heard Professor Lev's parting words—"Be very careful, Stefan!"

The corridor outside Professor Lev's door opened directly onto a sunny lounge area. Mustard-colored chairs and couches were scattered informally about the room. Here, the more favored inhabitants of the Stovlatz Station came to read or chat.

Stefan was happy to see that only one grouping of furniture was occupied. A plump, middle-aged scientist was sprawled out on a couch, leafing through a magazine. Stefan was sure that he could pass behind him unnoticed and proceed to the hallway that continued on the other side of the lounge. From where he stood, Stefan could see that it took a sharp right-angle turn. Then it became part of the dormitory wing where he was quartered. In just a few minutes he would be home free.

His mind leaped ahead to speculate on what he would find there. Why had somone falsely signed him into his room? Would that person still be there to explain? Or was this some kind of a trick to catch him out of bounds again?

Stefan was brought sharply to an awareness of present danger by a deep voice that sounded only a few meters from the room he had just passed.

"Sorry, sir!" it said respectfully, "I hope I haven't disturbed you. Just a routine inspection, you know."

A door shut firmly, and Stefan could hear the caretaker's remote control communicator bleep in a check-point notification to the security desk.

The boy did not look back but increased his speed. With luck he would cross that lounge well ahead of the caretaker. But could he take the risk? No, deep within himself he knew that time was critical—he *had* to get back to his room now!

On impulse he ducked into a waiting transportube and pressed the selector panel. As the cylindrical box turned on its axis and began to fall, Stefan gave a deep sigh.

This would take him a little out of his way, but it was safer. Once in the underground storage area, he wasted no time. He mingled with a group of workers carrying chemical supplies, working his way swiftly to the end of the passage. Here he darted around the corner and caught the transportube back to his own wing.

With a wild thrill of anticipation, Stefan raced down the hall to his bedroom. Just before jamming the key into his lock, he stopped to contain himself. Perhaps, after all, the guard had simply made a mistake in his report. Maybe the bed covers were bunched up and it only looked like someone was lying there. Or maybe...

He turned the key and threw his weight against the door. It opened abruptly and Stefan stumbled into the room, blinking in the dim light. Yes! *Someone was there, in his bed!* He snapped open the blinds. Sunlight fell across the coverlet in a revealing glare.

"What do you want?" a sleepy voice asked. There was a slight movement, and one amber eye peered out from under the covers.

"Oh, it's you!" The boy in the bed leaped nimbly to his feet. "I thought you'd never get back!"

Stefan stood dumbly, staring, while the other boy chattered on. Every feature of that face was known to him—the black hair growing well back from a high forehead; the gold-flecked amber eyes; even the ears were tipped slightly forward like Stefan's.

"If only you knew how I've been waiting for this moment!" the boy continued. "It's almost like looking in the mirror, isn't it?"

Prickly tears suddenly blurred Stefan's sight. "You are Evonn," he said.

The boy smiled. "Yes, I'm Evonn—and you are Stefan, and we are probably the only clone-brothers in the whole world. It takes some getting used to, doesn't it?" He allowed just two seconds of silence for getting used to the idea and then went rattling on. "I was beginning to think I'd never get through to you, especially after you found my open space in the Barrier and almost ruined everything."

"*Your* space in the Barrier? cried Stefan. "You mean that you had something to do with that hole I went through?"

"I sure did. It was a work of genius. For the past few weeks I've been wild to get through that Barrier and explore over here. My chance came when the guards finally let me in the computer room. They've been extra nice to me lately because I've been sick. I kept fooling around in there until I found a way to bend some of the lasers. But then you came along and went through the opening before I had a chance."

"Did you see me that day?" asked Stefan eagerly. "I banged on the window glass and yelled, but I couldn't tell if you saw me."

Evonn plopped down at the foot of the bed. "I knew something was happening but I couldn't see a thing. The next day the caretakers were in an uproar. I overheard them talking. It seems that the one who hit you was discharged. His boss said it was because of brutality, but the others knew it was because he'd seen too much."

"I thought that guy seemed shocked when he caught a look at both of us." said Stefan.

"He sure was. I heard him say that I had some kind of a twin. But he knew from your identity badge that our last names were different. 'Stefan Yanov,' he said. And then Dr. Zorak came over and made a big fuss. When I heard that, I asked a lot of questions. No one realizes how much those caretakers pick up.

But nothing made much sense until I got hold of a text on genetics research. Even then I had to piece together a dozen clues."

"And you had to come over and find out for yourself! But how did you get through today? They're checking out the Barrier system right now, and the whole area is crawling with guards."

"Exactly," said Evonn. With a dramatic gesture, he reached under Stefan's covers and whipped out the red-and-gray uniform coat of a guard. "I, er... borrowed this from a sleeping friend," he said.

Stefan whistled through his teeth admiringly. "That must have been some trip!"

"True, but our complex isn't as security-conscious as yours. Ours is used mostly as a conference center and public relations facility. Things are really grim over here. At first I was afraid I wouldn't be able to find your room. But the directory downstairs is just like ours."

"So you rolled up the hat and jacket knowing that whoever saw you would just assume you were me, right?"

"Right. That woman at the security desk gave me a big friendly smile." Evonn examined Stefan with a critical eye. "You know, we don't look *exactly* alike. We have the same hair and ears, and the crazy gold-sparked eyes, but..." He rose and pulled Stefan over to the mirror. "Look. You're a good inch taller than I am, and heavier, too. How can that be? Clones are supposed to be exactly alike."

Stefan studied their reflections in the glass. "I guess the difference is due to environmental influences—you know, how and where we were brought up."

"That must be the reason. But how did you get those big arm muscles? Do you lift weights?"

Stefan was amazed at the thin arms that Evonn held up for comparison. "No, but I used to live on a farm. In fact, I work on different farms every harvest season. Don't you?"

Evonn laughed. "A farm? Are you serious? I've never even seen the inside of a barn. I go to a boarding school in the west country. That's where I'd be right now if I hadn't gotten sick with a strep throat." He paused. "Hey, that might be why I'm smaller—I had rheumatic fever a couple of times when I was younger. Now, whenever I get a sore throat, I have to go on special medication and practically live in the infirmary."

"Rheumatic fever must be a contagious disease then," said Stefan. "Because if it was genetically caused, I would have had it, too."

"Well, it starts with a strepococcal infection and that's contagious, all right. It went through our dorm like wildfire six years ago. Up until then I was never sick. We must have been impossible to tell apart in those days."

Stefan jumped up. "I have a photo of myself when I was two. I'll show it to you."

He opened his closet door. There he paused as a thought struck him.

"Hey, Evonn. I've been dreaming a lot lately about being sick...and I also dreamed about doing some fancy stuff on a computer. Do you think it's possible...?"

Evonn looked up with interest. "You mean that you sort of 'experienced' some of the things I was involved in?"

"Maybe. They were such real dreams! Why were you shooting that laser gun, though—and marching out on the steppes?"

Now Evonn looked surprised. "Big guns? Troop duty?" He grinned. "You really must be crazy—and I'll never own up to being like you again. Find that photo and give your imagination a rest."

Stefan knelt and began to rummage in a large canvas bag at the back of the closet.

"Unless you're a lot neater than I am, you'll never find it," said Evonn.

Stefan laughed. "Give me a few weeks—it's in here some-where."

Suddenly Evonn stiffened. "Sh-h," he hissed, listening intently.

Footsteps sounded in the hall. They were headed towards Stefan's room. Instantly, both boys dived for cover.

Evonn threw himself flat on the bed and pulled up the blankets.

Stefan squeezed to the back of the closet and was just closing the door when a passkey rattled and the door to his room opened.

STEFAN got a whiff of a medicinal smell and then saw the staff physician pass by the open crack in the closet door. She was followed by a burly caretaker. They walked directly over to the bed where Evonn was pretending to sleep.

"There, you see?" she said. "I told you he would be here."

"I wasn't the one who reported him upstairs, Doctor," said the caretaker. "It was a caretaker on the research scientists' wing. They get jumpy up there sometimes with so many V.I.P.s around."

The doctor leaned over the bed. "How do you feel, Stefan?" she asked, pulling at the blankets.

"Can't you just leave me alone for awhile?" Evonn whined. He burrowed down further into the bedclothes. "Every time I fall asleep, someone comes bursting in and wakes me up."

In the closet, Stefan held his breath. If she insisted on examining her patient, she would notice at once the missing welt on his neck.

"Let me take your pulse," she demanded. "You look pale— what I can see of you."

"I have a terrible headache. Please let me go back to sleep. I'll come down before dinner and you can give me a thorough checkup then."

The doctor hesitated. "Well...all right then. Be at my office promptly at 1800."

She turned to the guard. "Register him in with a 'Don't Disturb' notation. He really should have some rest."

The caretaker touched his cap respectfully and they both left the room.

Stefan waited for several minutes before he dared to come

out of the closet. Then he tiptoed over to the bed and in high falsetto tones imitated the doctor. "Poor boy, he is *so* tired!"

Evonn sat up at once with a pleased smile on his face. "I was rather good, wasn't I?" he said. "They didn't suspect a thing!"

Stefan found that his legs were trembling, and he sat down on the bed so Evonn wouldn't notice.

"To tell the truth," Evonn admitted, "I was scared. If they had ever found out, we'd really be in trouble."

"But why?" asked Stefan. "I don't understand why they are so anxious to keep us apart!"

"I've been wondering about that, too. We are being raised and educated in such different ways. There I am in a boarding school with a million other boys, studying political science, economics, history, language, and things. And you are here alone with..." he waved his hand toward Stefan's microscope and technical books "...all this science stuff."

"Wait a minute," said Stefan slowly, "I just remembered something Dr. Zorak said. The plan is that we are to work somehow as a team in the government when we grow up."

"All right!" Evonn was all enthusiasm. "We'll make a great team, you and I! But...all the more reason for us to grow up together. We're so alike, I bet we'd even get to know what the other one was thinking."

"You mean mental telepathy—ESP?"

"Sure! After all, brain waves are measurable electrical impulses. Since our brains are identical, our impulse patterns must be sympathetic. I'm certain that we can learn to transmit mental messages."

Recalling some of the events of the past few weeks, Stefan answered, "I think we have already, Evonn. Even though we weren't even aware of it. But maybe that's the kind of thing Zorak is trying to prevent by keeping us apart. Maybe he doesn't want us to learn to develop any special abilities."

Evonn got up and walked to the window, his eyes bright with excitement.

[37]

"Of course, that's what he's afraid of. He wouldn't want us to get beyond his control. He'd want us to work well together but still be loyal only to him. It seems to me he intends to use us but would never really trust us."

"I doubt if Dr. Zorak trusts anybody. I think he wants all the power for himself," Stefan said. "Just suppose we never even met until we were adults. By then we might be so different that we wouldn't ever have a really close relationship."

Evonn grinned and broke in, "You mean a really 'clone' relationship!"

Suddenly they were both laughing. Stefan snatched up his pillow and pressed it against his face to stifle the noise. Evonn grabbed the sheet and tried to stuff it in his mouth. That only made them laugh harder.

Stefan sobered up first. He wiped his eyes and sighed. "I didn't really want to believe this cloning bit before." he said, "I felt so strange and so…abnormal; you know what I mean?"

Evonn nodded his head. "Yes, I know. Who could know better?"

"But now that I've met you," Stefan continued, "everything is different. Only we will have to be awfully careful for awhile. I'll have to calm Dr. Zorak's fears somehow about what I may have seen of you from the observation cubicle."

"And I had better get out of here." Evonn checked his timepiece. "The patrol is to leave at 1700, and I have to pass through with them."

"Evonn, aren't you afraid that they'll find out that you fouled up the Barrier from the computer terminals?"

Evonn assured him that with such a complex machine, it would be difficult to pin down just where the malfunction had occurred.

"One thing before you leave," Stefan said rapidly, "we have to think of a way to exchange messages. Who knows when we'll get to see each other again." He considered several possibilities and decided on the simplest. "This place is loaded

with shale. Let's attach a note to the underside of a flat rock
and scale it through the Barrier. The laser beams only react to
heat, so both the stone and paper are safe."

"That should work," said Evonn, "be sure to scale it through
near where the 'hole' was. I'll be looking for something from
you soon." Evonn paused at the door. "Good-bye for now,
brother."

Stefan grasped his shoulders and they embraced solemnly.

As the door closed behind Evonn, Stefan murmered, "Good-
bye, Evonn, I wonder if I'll ever see you again."

# CHAPTER 9

IT was dinnertime before Stefan's excitement began to wane. 'By now,' he reflected, 'Evonn should be safely back in his quarters. I'd better get down to the physician's office before she comes charging up after me.'

As he passed the cafeteria, the muted clatter of dishes and the low hum of voices attracted him. From the doorway he looked inside the dimly lit room. Small groups of men and women were seated at a dozen or so scattered tables, now spread with stiff white cloths. Long-stemmed wine glasses and a haze of cigarette smoke marked the main social hour at the Research Station.

A young technician with bushy hair glanced briefly at Stefan, and, without a sign, returned to his conversation with two comrades.

Stefan realized that in spite of having lived a month at this station, he was still an outsider. A familiar flush of anxiety rose inside him. Would he ever be accepted? This place was different from the other educational centers he'd been to. Here his world was peopled only by adults, all deeply involved in their own pursuits.

Oh, well, he had been alone before. In fact, he preferred to be.

Then with a burst of happiness, Stefan knew he need never try to convince himself of that again. Now he knew about Evonn, and now that fearful sense of aloneness could not strike at him as it had before.

Silently he surveyed the scene before him. 'Go ahead and ignore me. I don't care anymore, for I have someone who is closer to me than anyone you could *ever* know!' He whirled on his heel and sauntered away.

"Stefan, Stefan!" a voice called after him. The boy turned to find Professor Lev hurrying toward him, dinner napkin fluttering at his waist.

"Stefan, my boy. I've been looking for you," he said as he caught up with him. "What happened this afternoon? Was someone in your room? Was it...?"

Stefan smiled warmly at his teacher. He had forgotten for a moment about this friend. In a low voice he rapidly described Evonn's visit.

When he had finished, Professor Lev frowned behind his thick glasses. "A foolhardy thing for him to do. There must be some powerful attraction between you two, to make you take such risks. Did Evonn get back before the Barrier was reactivated?"

"I watched from the upper hall window. There was no trouble, so I'm sure he got through with the returning guards."

"But, Stefan, by now they will know that the source of the power failure wasn't at the Barrier itself. Won't they find out that Evonn had been experimenting with the control computer?"

Stefan shook his head. "Evonn says that the computer has malfunctioned before. He's safe unless the guards admit they let him into the computer room."

"They'll never confess to that," said Professor Lev, "not if they value their necks!"

"That's what I think, too, but I wish I could find out for sure!" Stefan's voice was tight with impatience. "I've *got* to find a way to get around outside this place so I can contact Evonn!"

Professor Lev put a warning hand on Stefan's arm and began talking quickly about his 'sore neck'. Over his shoulder, Stefan saw the physician walking directly towards them.

As soon as she caught sight of Stefan, she stopped short, motioning him to her side.

"So there you are!" she said, frowning. "You are late. I was just going to send a caretaker up after you."

She looked at Professor Lev as if to ask what he was doing with her patient.

"How fortunate that you came along, Doctor," he said calmly. He removed the napkin from his belt and patted his mouth with it. "I was just having dinner when young Stefan here passed the doorway of the cafeteria. He looked so pale that I stopped him to inquire about that nasty blow he suffered yesterday!"

"Ah, you know about that!" The physician seemed annoyed. "We are checking him out thoroughly. In fact, he should be in my office right now!"

"Excellent. The boy seems to be having a bad reaction to some 'muscle relaxant' you administered. Have you mentioned this to Dr. Zorak?"

The physician stiffened at this criticism of her treatment. "I am perfectly capable of handling my own affairs, thank you."

Professor Lev shrugged. "Well then, Stefan. I shall leave you in these capable hands. Good night."

"Good night, Professor Lev. Thank you for coming to my rescue," Stefan said.

As the professor walked away, the physician turned sharply to Stefan. "What do you mean, your 'rescue'?"

Taking his cue from Professor Lev's remark, Stefan enlarged his complaints.

"Well, I felt so dizzy a few minutes ago, I thought I was going to faint. I leaned against the wall by the cafeteria, and that's when the professor saw me and came to help."

The doctor seemed anxious to get Stefan out of sight. She took his elbow and began to propel him rapidly down the hall to her office.

"Not so fast!" he protested. "My headache will come back. I finally got rid of it after you let me sleep this afternoon. But what crazy nightmares I had!"

"So you had bad dreams, did you?" she guided him to a chair and pressed a thermometer against his inner arm. "Sometimes we must repeat shocking experiences in our sleep. It helps us to understand them. What did you dream about?"

Stefan eyed her warily. Seeming to misunderstand her, he answered. "There isn't much to tell about that experience. When the Barrier broke down, I went through just to see what was on the other side. But I hardly had a chance to do any exploring. All I saw was a boy with his head buried in a book. I didn't even get to talk to him—some caretaker sneaked up behind me and practically chopped my neck in two!"

Stefan noticed the physician's intent expression as he spoke of the other boy. 'Good,' he thought, 'now go tell Zorak that I didn't get a good look at anyone.'

The physician marked his temperature on a chart and examined his neck. "That was an unfortunate incident, Stefan. However, it was no more than you might expect. You did deliberately go out of bounds," she said coolly. "But I was asking you about the nightmares you had. Often just talking about them is a help."

The physician was clearly after information, and Stefan decided to give her an earful. He launched into a tale that combined every bad dream he'd ever had.

"...and then," said Stefan, finishing up with a few details from a book he'd once read "I dreamed that the whole world folded in around me. The sky sifted down and clogged my nostrils with cold, blue fog, and that mountainside split and thundered down around me so I couldn't move! And it all got so heavy...and I could feel my ribs cracking...and I was crushed!"

"I see." The physician's face was serious. "Do you often have these nightmares, Stefan?"

"Only since I've come to Stovlatz," he answered. "Sometimes I feel awfully cooped up here with all the barriers around. But it was probably that injection you gave me that caused the nightmare!"

The physician hastily steered the conversation in another

direction. "I imagine your daily study schedule here doesn't allow you much time for fresh air and exercise. Perhaps we can arrange something for you. Do you know that the young technicians here have an excellent basketball team?"

Stefan thought quickly. This might be a real opportunity. "I'm not much for team sports, Doctor," he said, "but I do enjoy jogging. You know, getting out there and really stretching my legs."

She hesitated a moment and then said, "I think we may be able to arrange that. Yes, with the proper equipment--er, shoes and so forth, I'm sure we can clear your request with head-quarters."

Stefan's hopes plummeted. 'Proper equipment!' he thought, 'that means those clothes will be so "bugged" they could trace me all the way to the moon in them.'

# CHAPTER  10

ALL morning Stefan waited impatiently to talk to Professor Lev. But as soon as he entered his instruction unit, he knew something was wrong.

Professor Lev's manner was unusually brisk. He gave Stefan no time to chat.

"Please be seated, Stefan. If we get right to work we may be able to make up the time you missed yesterday."

Cautiously, Stefan framed a question that would have a double meaning to the Professor.

"When shall I give you my report, sir? Some unexpected results have shown up, and I'd like to discuss them with you."

"Perhaps later, Stefan." Professor Lev shot him a warning glance. "Right now I want to show you a film on the winter acclimatization of warm-blooded animals. It will help you to understand the changes in blood chemistry experienced by our cosmonauts in the low-temperature modules."

He plugged a portable projector unit into an outlet on his desk and snapped open the screen. The voice of the film lecturer filled the room.

Professor Lev stood beside the desk with his back to the observation booth. Ignoring the film, he began to talk in a barely audible voice.

"Keep you eyes on the screeen," he said, "but listen to me. As you have guessed, we are being observed today. This sound unit, however, is directly above the transmitter to the observation booth. They can't hear my voice up there."

Stefan riveted his eyes straight in front of him, afraid that they would stray upward and give him away.

"It seems clear, Stefan," the Professor hurried on, "that Dr.

Zorak and I are headed for a major clash. He knows that I don't agree with his methods, and so he doesn't trust me. I must get away from here before he can trump up some official evidence against me."

The bright images on the screen swam before Stefan's eyes. He struggled to control the panic that rose inside him.

Professor Lev's low voice continued. "Within this station, Zorak has complete authority. It will be increasingly difficult for me to help you. But on the outside I, too, have some influence."

Stefan gathered his wits together. He pointed to the screen as if he were asking a question about the film, and said, "Perhaps if Dr. Zorak realizes that Evonn and I already know about being clones, we can work something out."

"No!" Professor Lev cut him off flatly. "This situation is far more complicated than you know. Dr. Zorak has gone to great lengths to hide his experiments in human cloning. He would never allow you and Evonn to get together until all his plans are ripe."

Professor Lev walked over to the animated screen and tapped it lightly, as if emphasizing a point made by the lecturer. Then he resumed his former position with his back to the observation window.

"And, Stefan, there is something else in Dr. Zorak's attitude that disturbs me. Something almost vengeful…"

The bleeper on the Professor's belt blared out, shrill and imperious.

"That will be Zorak now," he said. "One last thing, Stefan. One of the caretakers is a friend. You will be contacted." He hurried to the back of the room and after a surprised apology spoken into the communicator, he returned to his desk and unpugged the film unit.

"There seems to be some electrical interference in the building," he said. "We shall have to view this film at another time."

The rest of the hour was filled with routine classroom work. After the work had been put away, Stefan went to his locker. As the physician had promised, a new pair of track shoes hung inside.

"Professer Lev," he called, "look at these—I'm taking up running. The physician told me I wasn't getting enough fresh air and exercise."

His teacher looked up from his books. "A good sport," he said. "It will keep you in shape. You do spend too much time indoors."

Stefan examined the shoes minutely as he put them on. He couldn't see any evidence of homing devices, but he was certain that they were there. 'It doesn't really matter,' he thought, 'if my jogging route works out as I planned it, I won't even need to go out of bounds.'

He laced the shoes swiftly and sprinted down the corridor to the security desk. Then he ran out into the bright spring sunlight. Overhead, the stark gray branches of the linden trees were softened by a yellow haze of unfurling leaves. Stefan's spirits lifted, and he set off on his carefully planned route.

As he neared the Barrier fenceline, Stefan felt in his pocket for his pencil and paper. Finally he would be able to send a note to Evonn. He began to scan the ground as he ran, looking for a flat rock. Since the entire complex was built on a natural vein of shale, he soon found what he was looking for. The rock was about the size and thickness of his hand. At his next rest stop, Stefan sat down and wrote his note.

> Dear E.—I jog at 0700, 1700, and 2100 hours. Trouble here. How goes it on your side? More later.
>
> Yours, S.

Stefan taped the note to the rock. Then he rose and set off toward the Barrier. Holding the shale flat, he scaled it through the invisible fence. As he had expected, the Barrier remained dormant to the cold rock. The rock skipped once in the damp grass and settled, note-side down, near the lower branches of a square-clipped bush.

Without breaking his stride, Stefan continued on his oval course.

"Come and get it, Evonn," he whispered. "Come now before something else goes wrong!"

# CHAPTER ● ● 11

As Stefan jogged back to the somber granite building his spirits sank with each step.

'How will I ever be able to stand this place if something happens to Professor Lev?' he wondered morosely. 'That poor guy could end up stacking stalactites in Siberia!'

By this time, Stefan began to feel the effects of his first run. His leg muscles were tight and his back ached. He decided to head straight for the shower. He stepped into the transportube and punched out the code for his floor. Just as the doors were closing, a caretaker stepped inside. She nodded to him in a friendly manner.

"I am Marya," she said. "I have something for you."

Stefan eyed her suspiciously. Marya? He didn't remember hearing that name before.

The woman's steady blue eyes met his unswervingly. "So," she said, "you don't know about me. I thought that Professor Lev had told you."

"Oh, yes!... but I didn't think... he just said 'a guard'," Stefan stammered, wishing desperately that conversation came more easily to him.

"I have something for you from the Professor," Marya said briskly. She handed him a brown media center envelope with the lesson number stamped on the outside.

"Thank you," Stefan said. "Excuse me, but I think I *have* seen you before."

Marya stared at him. "I should think you have! I am posted at the caretaker station on your floor."

Stefan flushed with embarrassment. He must have passed her every day that he'd been at Stovlatz. Yes, now he could even remember thinking vaguely that she reminded him of his old nurse, Tonia. They had the same square, sturdy figure and broad cheekbones of some ancient Magyar heritage.

"I'm sorry," he murmured. "I guess I just don't look closely at faces. All my life, the people around me have changed so often that I don't pay much attention anymore."

Marya's expression mellowed. "I understand," she said softly.

The transportube stopped at Stefan's floor and Marya joined the other caretaker at the central desk. Stefan hurried off to his room with his package pressed against his side.

Inside, he took a long cartridge of microfiche from the envelope and inserted it into his desk viewer. He focused the machine on the title of what looked to be an ordinary monograph. It read: PRESERVING LIFE THROUGH THE CONTINUUM OF TIME AND SPACE.

Stefan slumped in his chair, weak with disappointment. That was last week's assignment. Could Professor Lev be that confused? It seemed unlikely. Stefan leaned forward again and read through the whole monograph, searching for some message from his friend. At the end there was a blank space, and, after a neat splice in the filmstrip, another article appeared. It looked to Stefan as if it had been photographed from a foreign newspaper.

He adjusted the focus for smaller print. Yes, it was from an old newspaper, datelined Budapest, more than a decade ago.

### SECRECY SURROUNDS FATE OF MISSING SCIENTIST

DR. GRIGORY METVEDENKO, RENOWNED SCIENTIST
AND MILITARY HERO, HAS BEEN REPORTED MISSING SINCE
LAST WEDNESDAY IN AN AIRCRAFT ACCIDENT IN THE
CARPATHIAN MOUNTAINS. A GUEST SPEAKER AT THE
UPCOMING INTERNATIONAL SCIENTIFIC SYMPOSIUM IN THIS

CITY, DR. METVEDENKO WAS FLYING EN ROUTE TO BUDAPEST
WHEN HIS SMALL PLANE APPARENTLY DEVELOPED ENGINE
TROUBLE AND WENT DOWN NEAR THE HUNGARIAN BORDER.
RESCUE OPERATIONS HEADED BY DR. IGOR ZORAK, OF THE
NATIONAL INSTITUTE OF SCIENCE, FAILED TO ASCERTAIN
THE FATE OF THE PILOT OR HIS PASSENGER.
ACCORDING TO SOURCES IN THE SCIENTIFIC
COMMUNITY, THERE IS REASON TO BELIEVE THAT DR.
METVEDENKO MAY HAVE BEEN ATTEMPTING TO DEFECT
FROM HIS NATIVE COUNTRY.

Stefan frowned, totally bewildered. 'That's got to be our Dr. Zorak,' he thought, 'but who is this Metvedenko?' He scanned the article again. In the column to the right of the article was a photograph. As it snapped into sharp focus on the glass screen before him, Stefan gasped.

Now there was no question in Stefan's mind who this man was. It was like seeing his own face some twenty years in the future.

The man was about thirty years old. His black hair was clipped short in a military cut and revealed large ears that tipped forward in an inquisitive fashion. His unusual light-colored eyes seem to look directly at Stevan.

"Dr. Grigory Metvedenko," Stefan whispered, "why did you want to be cloned?"

# CHAPTER  12

FOR the next few days Stefan was very quiet. He spent long hours in the media center absorbing backround material on his new assignment from Professor Lev. Aside from Marya, he did not see a friendly face for four days.

'Life was a lot simpler in the days of the old Stefan,' he thought, 'but a lot more lonely, too.'

Although he had exchanged several notes with Evonn, he hadn't yet found a way to tell him about Metvedenko. It was too hard to explain in a brief message.

As he passed the security desk in the hall one afternoon, Marya stopped him.

"I'm glad you came by, Stefan," she said. "We have just received a message for you from Dr. Zorak. He wishes to see you immediately."

"He does? Right now?" Stefan's voice rose and broke off in a ragged squeak.

She nodded. "Just keep your wits about you, Stefan."

Stefan took a deep breath and stepped into the waiting transportube. Suddenly he began to have second thoughts about his rebellious activities. Until now his whole life had been built around being a good student and a hard worker. But now he was involved in acts that were clearly against the will of the authorities who paid for his support. Had Zorak found out what he was up to? What would he do to him if he had?

By the time the transportube reached the ground floor, Stefan was really nervous. As he stood outside Dr. Zorak's office and gave his name, he was almost afraid that the transmitter would pick up the wild pounding of his pulses.

The doors slid open and Dr. Zorak motioned Stefan to enter his study. It was the same room in which Stefan had so recently overheard this man threaten Professor Lev, and where he had learned that he himself was the subject of genetic experimentation.

A wave of nausea swept over the boy, and he sat quickly in one of two chairs placed in front of a round glass fireplace.

"Good afternoon, Stefan." Dr. Zorak crinkled his eyes in a joyless smile. "At last we can have a nice, long talk." He seated himself in the opposite chair.

Even as Stefan answered politely, he thought to himself, 'I do not like you, Dr. Zorak. You should not get away with pushing people around the way you do.'

The tall, thin man leaned forward in his chair and assumed an air of sincerity. "I don't know whether you realize it, Stefan, but you are very important to us here. When you were just a tiny lad, we looked you over and gave you some tests and decided that you were special. Even though you were a penniless orphan, we decided to give you the best education in the most up-to-date learning centers in the country."

He looked searchingly at Stefan. "You know that this is true, don't you?"

Stefan reacted with an automatic, "Yes, sir." Perhaps he was only in for a you-should-be-grateful lecture, after all. He would have liked to point out a few details that Zorak had left out of his penniless orphan biography.

"However, Stefan," Dr. Zorak continued, "there has been a change in your attitude lately. We have detected a certain lack of cooperation, a tendency to retreat into yourself. And I think I know the reason why."

"You know the reason why?" echoed the boy.

"Yes. I think it relates to your adventures last week when the Barrier malfunctioned That was a freak accident, I grant you, but against all regulations you..."

Dr. Zorak stopped. Evidently he was veering off onto the wrong track. When he spoke again, his voice was friendly once more. "It was a freak accident, and I can't say that I blame you

for taking advantage of it. We all admire an inquiring young mind like yours."

Stefan almost choked at this hypocrisy. "Is that why you put a directional signal on my belt?" he burst out. "And is that why your caretaker knocked me unconcious and the physician gave me some kind of a truth drug—because you admire an inquiring young mind?"

Instantly Stefan felt like biting off his tongue. This was no time to enrage Dr. Zorak. But to his surprise the director merely raised his eyebrows.

"So, Stefan," he purred, "you are neither as passive nor as unobservant as you seem. However, your understanding is severely limited. This is a military installation as well as a research center. Some of our experiments are dangerous. They are also top secret. Boundary limitations are for our own protection as well as for security reasons. Everyone here wears a belt like the one you have." He flipped open his jacket to show Stefan that he, too, wore one.

Stefan's hands gripped the arms of his chair. He felt that he had lost a great deal in this game of wits. Dr. Zorak had tricked him into blurting out his resentment and had shrewdly defended his own actions with one simple explanation. Stefan planned his next move carefully. He must pretend to believe Dr. Zorak's explanations. As proof of his new faith, Stefan himself would bring up the most delicate question of all.

"I guess I shouldn't have made such a fuss about the security regulations," Stefan said. "But what about the other building complex? What about that other boy I saw?"

"Ah, now, Stefan," the director answered smoothly, "I was hoping you wouldn't ask about him!"

Stefan struggled to keep an expression of wide-eyed innocence. "Why not? I just about got a look at him, when— blam! that caretaker knocked me out. There are no other kids my age around her. Why can't I talk to him?"

Dr. Zorak rose and took a photograph out of his desk

drawer. He handed it to Stefan, watching him closely.

Stefan could scarcely control his relief when he saw the picture. Now he knew what Dr. Zorak was up to. Although the boy in the photograph was about thirteen, he was clearly not Evonn. His hair was curly, his ears tiny, and his whole expression was one of chronic discontent.

"That boy is not a suitable friend for you, Stefan," the director said at last. "He has a strange neurological problem we've been working on for several years. Frankly, I've begun to lose hope for him."

"Is that why his presence is such a big secret?"

Dr. Zorak nodded. "We don't think it necessary to advertise our failures." He leaned back in his chair. "I'm glad we've had this talk, Stefan. I hope it has served to answer your questions."

"Oh, it has, sir."

"Now I'm going to tell you something that few other people know." The older man lowered his voice in a confidential manner. "I knew your father well years ago. He was one of the most brilliant men I have ever known. When I was Director of Research and Development at N.S.I., he worked with me for several years. He had a great career before him, until he lost sight of the fact that the advance of science is an end in itself."

For a moment Dr. Zorak was lost in his own thoughts. Unpleasant ones, Stefan decided, as he saw the frown that folded deep into the man's forehead.

"Well," Dr. Zorak returned to his point abruptly, "at any rate there was an accident and we lost him." He got up from his chair. "We'll talk about this again, Stefan. Today my schedule is extremely tight."

"I hope we do," returned Stefan eagerly. "I never knew anyone who knew my father before."

As the sliding panels of the door closed behind him, Stefan heaved a great sigh of relief. 'That man is a clever fox,' he thought. 'If I hadn't actually talked to Evonn face to face, I would have believed every word he said!'

In the hallway, Stefan met Marya returning from her security rounds. He fell into step beside her.

"No," she said, "don't walk with me. Meet me at the desk and speak only if no one is nearby."

Stefan dropped back immediately. He stooped down and re-tied his shoelace. By the time he finished, Marya had reached the desk. The other caretaker started off on his rounds.

As Stefan approached, Marya looked up anxiously from the forms she was filling out.

"What did Dr. Zorak want with you?" she asked.

Stefan was surprised at her direct question. Dr. Lev had told him to trust Marya, but he had no idea how much she knew. He hesitated.

Marya smiled understandingly. "You are right to be cautious," she said. "Professor Lev and I are old friends. His work in nuclear medicine once saved my life. But now he is deeply concerned about you and your situation here!" She glanced about nervously. "We are all in this place because Dr. Zorak likes to surround himself with those he can manipulate."

Stefan nodded. "I am beginning to realize that. But what hold does he have over you?"

"My husband was the editor of a dissident newspaper," she answered. "He is now in prison. Dr. Zorak is also the chief psychiatrist on the prison review board. For three years he has promised to help us."

"So you wait, and you cooperate," Stefan whispered.

Marya changed the subject. "But what of you?" she asked. "Why did Dr. Zorak call you down for a personal interview?"

"He wanted to convince me that everything that goes on around here is perfectly normal and," he shuddered, "I think he wants me to like him."

Marya's sturdy frame relaxed. "Well, then, he has no idea how much you already know. And he would, of course, want you to like him. Your willing cooperation is essential to his plans."

"He almost fooled me, Marya. He put on a big sincerity act and told me a story that was such a clever blend of the truth and lies that I almost believed him."

"He would be good at that!" Marya went back to filling out her forms. "You had better go now. Long conversations can be dangerous."

Stefan was sorry that their talk was ended, but he knew she was right to be cautious.

By the time Stefan could get to his evening run, he was several minutes late. All the while he was changing into his jogging clothes, he sent urgent mental messages to his brother. 'Evonn—contact me...I have important news...I must reach you!' This time Stefan tried a new technique. He closed his eyes and pictured each word moving across his inner vision, like a line of teletype.

The night air was oppressive. Overhead, dark clouds were gathering, causing an early dusk. As he set out at a brisk pace, Stefan thought over Evonn's last note. It had been a jumble of good news and bad news. Good, that his medical checkup showed him clear of infection. Bad, that the friendly attitude of the caretakers in his complex had changed since the breakdown of the Barrier. They were very strict now and wouldn't let Evonn near the computer room anymore.

As Stefan neared the invisible Barrier, he located two key bushes and stayed well to one side of them. His eyes swept the grass as he ran, but he found no messages. His disappointment at this was so keen he could taste it.

Suddenly a low voice called out, "I say, there's a familiar face!"

Stefan froze as a shadow detached itself from a low bush on

the other side of the Barrier. It was Evonn!

"What are you doing out here now?" whispered Stefan. "I can't even stop to talk to you. Someone might notice it on the tracking screen."

"But we need to talk," said Evonn. "I went to bed early and suddenly I knew you were worried and wanted to tell me something important."

"That's true. I did send you a mental message—but I was expecting a note. Wait here a minute. I have an idea that might buy us some time."

Stefan ran on until he was well away from the Barrier. Quickly he stripped to his underclothes. Although he was sure that the homing devices were in his belt and shoes, he spread his whole jogging costume on the ground as if he were resting.

'Maybe they'll think I stopped to rest and just fell asleep,' he thought. 'That should give us about five minutes until they send someone out after me.' The stiff grass prickled his tender feet as he sprinted back.

Evonn smiled when he saw Stefan approaching. "Well, I guess that outfit could be called the 'bare essentials'. But my own isn't much better."

"Why, what do you have on?"

"Not much." Evonn admitted. "I've been extra careful lately just in case they are tracking me, too. I took off every stitch and lowered myself out the window on this blanket. Then I used it for a wrap."

If he hadn't been so frightened, Stefan would have laughed at the black, shrouded figure whose skinny bare legs gleamed in the half-light.

"We don't have much time," he warned. "First, what's happening over on your side?"

Evonn sobered immediately. "Here's something I stole for you." He folded a sheet of white paper into an airplane and sailed it across to Stefan. "It's a schematic drawing of the entire Barrier network."

Stefan studied the broad black lines in silence.

"I never had a clear idea of the layout of this place before," he said at last. "I knew there were three main complexes, but I didn't realize that the Military-Central security area was so big. Too bad we don't know someone over there. You know all about the Public Relations Complex, and I know about Research—if we had a friend there, we'd know what was going on all over the place."

"Not much chance of that," said Evonn. "Those guys aren't at all friendly. They're all a bunch of super-soldiers. They monitor the security systems that monitor us, you know."

"Yeah. I guess they take care of that Outer Barrier, too," said Stefan, studying the drawing. "That's something I never knew about before. The security around here is incredible—each complex surrounded by its own Inner Barrier, and then an Outer Barrier that goes around the outside of the whole station!"

"Can you imagine someone trying to break into this place? Even with a map it's impossible to figure exactly where those Barriers begin. You can't see a thing."

Stefan took a last look at the map and tore it into tiny pieces which he scattered and pushed under the sod.

"Time is running out, Evonn," he said. "I've got to tell you what I've found out. First, listen to this newspaper article that Professor Lev got through to me." He recited the article from memory.

When he finished, Evon spoke up impatiently. "What does that have to do with us? The only name I recognized was Dr. Zorak's."

"Just tell me what you make of it, Evonn. I'm afraid I may be reading too much into it." Stefan repeated the article.

"Well, it seems to me," said Evonn, "that this guy, Metvedenko, decided to defect. Somehow his plans are discovered and his plane goes down. It happens every day—so what?"

"Why do you suppose Dr. Zorak was involved?" asked Stefan. Doesn't it seem strange that a professor from the Science Institute should lead a mountain rescue team?"

"Not if he were Metvedenko's good friend," said Evonn, "... or maybe his worst enemy."

"That's the point, Evonn," Stefan said breathlessly. "I found out that Metvedenko had been his special protegé. That means when Metvedenko defected, he walked out on Zorak's whole project. That must have left Dr. Zorak looking foolish."

Evonn shivered and drew his blanket close about him. "I get it— the plane didn't actually crash. It managed to get down somehow. So Dr. Zorak had to be sure that Metvedenko was either killed or captured."

"That's what I think, too," said Stefan quietly. "But I know something more about Metvedenko. "Shut your eyes and concentrate, Evonn. I want you to try to see a photograph that was with the article!"

There was complete silence, then Evonn whispered, "That man was our clone-father, wasn't he, Stefan? I can't really 'see' him, but I can tell what you are thinking about the photo."

"He looks just like us, Evonn. I'm sure he was our 'father'. At least you picked up that much of what I was thinking," said Stefan. "You did quite well with the ESP. We're going to need it. Dr. Zorak doesn't have any intention of letting us get together for some time." He told Evonn about his interview with Dr. Zorak.

Evonn was furious. "So he tried to trick you into thinking I didn't exist! You know, we're just a pair of lab mice to him— breed them, train them, and watch them perform!"

Later, as Stefan lay in the grass waiting to be found by the caretaker, he was haunted by Evonn's image of white mice in a cage. He could see himself scrambling through the educational maze prepared for him, peered at, and prodded by the ever-watchful Dr. Zorak.

# CHAPTER 14

"PROFESSOR LEV!" called Stefan as he burst into the instruction unit the next morning. "I'm early today, do you think..."

The man at the microscope looked up. He had short, curly hair and a face lined with anxiety. He was a complete stranger.

"Where is Professor Lev?" asked Stefan, his heart sinking.

"I am Professor Eisenberg," the man said, "and you must be Stefan Yanov. Although Professor Lev is no longer here, we will continue your studies as scheduled." He indicated that Stefan should be seated.

"But where is Professor Lev?" repeated Stefan.

Professor Eisenberg coughed nervously. "Dr. Zorak is the administrative head of this project," he said. "I suggest that you refer your questions to him at the end of class."

Stefan dropped into his seat and stared numbly at the desk in front of him.

Professor Eisenberg opened Stefan's lab report and began to discuss it with him.

Stefan couldn't concentrate on his lesson. He managed to make an appropriate "yes" or "no" whenever his teacher's voiced paused, but his mind was whirling. 'What has Zorak done now? Has he sent Professor Lev to a labor camp? Will I ever see him again?'

At last Professor Eisenberg closed the notebook and said, "That will be all today, Stefan. The next experiment, as you have seen, will require a great deal of time in the lab. If you keep in mind the points we've discussed today, you won't have any trouble with it."

Stefan, who hadn't heard a word for the past half an hour, assured the Professor that he understood the procedure thoroughly. He grabbed his notes and was out of the class before his teacher had risen from his chair.

Stefan went back to his own wing looking for Marya, but she was nowhere to be seen. He returned to his room in hopes of finding a last minute note from Professor Lev, but there was nothing. 'Do I dare to go down and ask Dr. Zorak about Professor Lev?' he wondered. 'No I can't do that. Others have come and gone and I haven't questioned it.'

Keeping to his usual schedule, Stefan went down to the cafeteria where he choked down a bowl of soup and then checked his daily assignments at the media center. After a wasted hour in the listening carrel, he realized that the English language was just not going to make sense to him that day. He put away the holographs and changed his clothes quickly. This was one day that he really needed to get outside and run!

The caretaker at the central desk looked surprised as Stefan approached him in his running outfit. He reviewed the daily computer printout and nodded curtly to the boy.

"I see that your schedule has been changed," he said.

"Some of it has," Stefan agreed. "My last two runs have been moved up a few hours. It seems that I fell asleep out there last night when I stopped to rest."

"Well, just be sure you're back inside at 1600 this time," the caretaker ordered.

Today not even the fragrant breeze blowing in from across the plains lifted Stean's spirits. 'Evonn will be upset about Professor Lev's disappearance, too,' he thought. 'He's the best friend we've got.'

As he neared the Barrier, Stefan's sense of apprehension grew to alarm. 'What's the matter with Evonn?' he wondered, 'I can just feel that he's upset. Surely he doesn't know about Professor Lev already.'

Alongside the second bush, Stefan saw a flat piece of shale lying in the grass. He turned it over and found that a message was taped to the bottom of it. He picked it up and ran on to his next rest stop.

The note was written in a shaky handwriting.

*Bad news, Stefan. I am being sent back to boarding school! The train arrives here at 0900 Wednesday. They told me that since I'm better and have made up the work I missed, there is no reason for me to stay here any longer. What can we do?*

*Evonn*

Stefan rolled over in the grass. Hot tears squeezed between his eyelids. He felt alone, empty, and defeated. Only a few short months ago he had prided himself on the fact that he really didn't need other people to make him happy. 'How could I have been so stupid,' he thought.

But Evonn's note hadn't sounded defeated. He had expected to *do* something.

Stefan sat up. 'There is only one thing left to do,' he decided. 'We must escape!'

# CHAPTER 15

At precisely 1600 Stefan checked in at the central desk. He nodded to the guard and went directly to his floor.

As he strode past the storage room, the door swung open. There was a rush of movement and a hand clasped firmly over his mouth. He was dragged backward into the small, airless room.

"Sh-h, don't make a sound!" a voice whispered.

The hand released him and he turned around to face Marya.

Stefan wiped the perspiration from his forehead. "Am I glad to see you!" he whispered. "I thought for a minute that Zorak had read my mind and was about to finish me off right here!"

"I'm sorry to be so rough, Stefan," Marya's voice was barely audible, "but I'm supposed to be off duty now, and the other caretaker will patrol this hall within the minute. Shhh."

They waited in breathless silence until a heavy tread outside the door indicated that the guard had passed by.

Marya led him between narrow rows of shelves stacked with supplies to the back of the room where a small, barred window let in a patch of daylight.

"Won't my homing devices show where I am?" he asked.

"No," answered Marya. "They don't work inside buildings."

Stefan looked surprised. "I must learn about all these things before Evonn and I can make our escape."

Marya's face paled. "Escape?" she echoed. "Then Professor Lev was right. He knew you would come to that decision."

"You saw Professor Lev?" cried Stefan. "When? Where? What has happened to him?"

Marya grasped his arm. "Keep your voice down," she warned, "you are not to worry. He has been transferred. His friend at the University managed to convince Dr. Zorak's superior that Professor Lev is essential to the success of an important new program."

Stefan's joy blazed—and died in an instant. "But he knows too much! Zorak can't take a chance that he'll tell what's going on here!"

"Don't be so innocent, Stefan," Marya said. "Dr. Zorak has powerful safeguards to insure Professor Lev's silence. Now, tell me how you plan to escape. This Station is guarded by ultramodern, ultrasensitive equipment."

Stefan shook his head in despair. "I don't know yet. But we have to find a way soon. Evonn is going to be sent away on Wednesday!"

"That leaves scarcely enough time to plan an escape, no less accomplish it! Can't you and Evonn find some way to live with this situation and wait for a better time to act?"

"Marya, there may never be a better time!" answered Stefan. "We don't want to be separated again, and we don't want to become Dr. Zorak's trained robots, either."

Marya stared out the window for a moment. Then she turned to Stefan. "You are determined, then, to make an attempt to escape?"

"We have to," he said simply. "Evonn and I have been moving toward this decision for some time. Without even realizing it, we've been preparing ourselves."

"Yes," she said, "I can see that this is so. Then I will tell you the rest of Professor Lev's message. I was to wait until after you had made a definite resolve to leave."

Stefan could sense a hesitancy on her part. It was almost as if she were afraid to go on.

"It concerns your clone-father," she said in a rush. "Professor Lev's friend at the University found the confidential report of the mountain rescue team led by Dr. Zorak thirteen years ago.

The report stated that by the time the rescue team found the crash site, no one was in the plane. It was badly damaged. Dr. Metvedenko's seat was covered with blood. A portion of his hand with an inscribed ring had been severed. Zorak's team searched for days but couldn't find either the pilot or Metvedenko."

Stefan broke in. "Slow down, Marya. Does this mean that they got away?"

"Either that, or they died somewhere in the attempt."

"But, Marya, I've figured out the dates involved. Evonn and I weren't cloned until after the date of the crash! Are you sure they weren't caught?"

"Yes, we're sure. This was an official report and was fully investigated," Marya said. "Professor Lev believes that Dr. Zorak was able to salvage more than enough of Metvedenko's living cells from the crash site to begin the cloning process!"

"Then poor Metvedenko didn't even know about it!" A flash of anger swept through Stefan. "And this man Zorak calls himself a leader! He's just a common thief! What could be worse than stealing a man's very genes?"

Marya again pressed her hand over Stefan's mouth. "You must control yourself! I was afraid you would react this way!"

Stefan shook off her hand. "What a rotten kind of revenge Dr. Zorak has planned. His career must have suffered when Metvedenko ran out on him. He no longer had his brilliant scientist; but then, even better—he got his clones! So now Zorak means to use Evonn and me to maneuver himself into a position of real power!"

"Stefan, listen to me!" Marya insisted. "I'm afraid you are right, but there is no time to dwell on that now. You must concentrate on planning and carrying out a most dangerous escape. Remember, Professor Lev can only help you after you are already outside the Barriers."

Stefan took a deep breath. "Yes, we have to get away from here. You can see that now. What is the rest of Professor Lev's message?"

"There are no details at this point. He is in contact with an underground network of dissidents who will get you away from here—fast and far. Providing, of course, you can produce a miraculous escape to the outside."

Stefan sighed. "That's just one part of the problem. First I'll have to figure out a miraculous escape from inside this building."

"I shall do everything I can to help you," Marya said quietly. "I know the Caretaker Patrol routes as well as the lines on my face."

Stefan felt a lump rising in his throat. "Oh, no, Marya. You'd be risking your life and your husband's safety, too!"

Abruptly, Marya turned away from him. Her body began to shake wth the force of stifled sobs.

Stefan stared at her dumbly. Was this the brisk and sturdy Marya of a moment ago? His stomach twisted with dread.

"What has happened? What's wrong, Marya?"

With a tremendous effort, Marya regained her self control. She coughed and sniffed and brusquely wiped the tears out of her eyes. "Professor Lev found another report in the files...it was about my husband." After an agonized silence she went on. "My husband died a year ago from malnutrition...in an isolation cell."

"Oh, no!" Stefan moaned. "Then Dr. Zorak wasn't doing anything for you—or him. He didn't even tell you?"

Marya shook her head wordlessly.

Stefan put an arm about her shoulder and in a hoarse whisper cursed the cruelty of Dr. Zorak.

# CHAPTER ● 16

STEFAN saluted the caretaker outside the lab window and slid onto a tall four-legged stool. The whole building was quiet, and here inside the lab only the rustling of white mice in their cages could be heard. The sun sparkled against orderly rows of bottles and test tubes.

Stefan relaxed and stretched, like a cat. He could almost feel himself settling down. This was his world. Here he would be able to think best. Flipping his notebook open, he checked his work sheet for the week. As was usual at the start of a new experiment, he was scheduled into the lab for large blocks of time. Now he had special plans for every second of that time!

He pulled his lab manual towards him and glanced at the familiar headings: Experiment No. _____, Purpose, Materials, Procedure, Observations, Conclusion.

'If I were being truthful,' he thought with a rueful smile, 'I would write—Purpose: To Find a Means of Escape. Materials: One cranium (my own) containing about 1.4 kilograms of gray matter. Procedure: Think, think, think! Observations: An impossible task. Conclusions: Doubtful.'

Stefan fought down a wave of panic. Perhaps he should start by writing down everything he had learned about the experimental station so far.

He seized his pencil and began with the diagram Evonn had shown him.

When he finished his drawing, he methodically set about to outline his knowledge of the security systems guarding the Station.

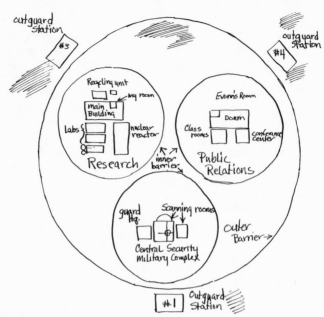

## Security Measures:

1. Inner Barriers controlled by computer within each complex. Inaccessible.
2. Outer Barrier controlled at the Central Security Complex. Inaccessible.

## Possible Means of Evading Barriers:

1. Going over it—need for special equipment such as balloon, airplane, etc.
2. Going under it—need for tunneling equipment and much time.
3. Going through it—need of access to computers. Now more heavily guarded than ever.

## Patrol Routes of Guards and Caretak....

The lab door swished open and footsteps clicked across the floor. Stefan looked up and saw to his horror that Dr. Zorak was striding towards him. Instantly, he leaped off the stool, managing to upset his notebook. It flipped over and landed on the floor, scattering papers in all directions.

"I seem to have startled you, Stefan," said Dr. Zorak.

"Yes, you d-did!" stammered Stefan. He knelt and began to gather his papers, carefully keeping his pencilled notes covered. "I was so involved in looking over Professor Eisenberg's notes that I didn't even hear the door open."

This answer seemed to please Dr. Zorak. "So, you find Professor Eisenberg a stimulating teacher?"

Stefan hesitated. "Professor Eisenberg is all right, but where is Professor Lev? Is he sick? Has he gone away?"

An expression of annoyance crossed Dr. Zorak's face. "Professor Lev proved to be unreliable," he said. "I have replaced him. Professor Eisenberg has a superior background in the area of low-temperature biology which you are about to study."

He opened Stefan's textbook and thumbed through the pages, stopping at one headed Space Cryobiology.

"You will find this most interesting, Stefan. In fact, your ... father did some of the pioneering work in this field."

"Really? May I see that, sir?" Stefan grasped the book and scanned the next few pages. "That's odd, I don't see his name metioned here."

It wasn't until Stefan saw the intense expression on Dr. Zorak's face that he realized what a dreadful error he had made. Dr. Zorak had never mentioned Metvedenko by name!

The tall man bent over Stefan and purred, "And just what name are you looking for, Stefan?"

Stefan's mind raced. "Well, my name is Yanov, so my father's must have been the same."

"Oh," Dr. Zorak straightened up again. "No, you were given the name of the family who reared you. Since you became a ward of the state, it simplified matters."

"I see," said Stefan, noting that Dr. Zorak still hadn't told him the name. "In what phase of cryobiology did my father work?"

"At the time, our government was experimenting with cryonic suspension modules. You have probably read about low-temperature holding chambers. They were designed to slow down the cosmonaut's aging processes during long-distance flight."

"Cryonic suspension modules?" repeated Stefan. "I've never heard of them."

"Although they proved to be inefficient, I was impressed with your father's work. When I was later selected to head a high-priority defense project, I requested that your father join me. It was a great opportunity."

"That must have been the big project you worked on together."

"In a way, yes. We were developing the famous L-beam Satellites," Dr. Zorak answered in a flat voice.

"I *have* read about those L-beamers," said Stefan. "They were called the 'killer satellites'! And to think that my own father developed them!"

Dr. Zorak stiffened angrily. "Hardly! The man de..." He caught himself midword and continued in a calmer voice. "Your father *decided* to attend an international science seminar during the early stages of our work. His plane crashed and he never came back."

Stefan avoided the Director's eyes. 'What you almost told me, Dr. Z.,' he thought, 'was that my father defected when he was forced to work on the most deadly space weapon yet invented.'

Out loud he said sorrowfully, "Yes, you had told me about his death. I guess that means the cryonic modules were his most significant contribution to science."

Dr. Zorak rose and brushed off his dark suit. "Yes, but even that project was discarded when the drug Vitadorm was discovered. Drugs can lower the temperature and slow the body functions more quickly and efficiently than external means."

Stefan drew in a sharp breath and coughed to cover it. Did this man realize what he was saying? He took a big chance. "I believe Professor Eisenberg referred to the change-over to cryobiological drugs. Where can I read about these experiments?"

"Oh, in the library," Dr. Zorak answered absently, and then,

"I want you to know, Stefan, that your father had a great potential. As a young man he served brilliantly in the Air Force, and when he came back to the University, I recognized immediately that his was an exceptional mind—undisciplined, but talented. You have that same potential, Stefan, plus the superb scientific education I have provided for you."

Stefan controlled an impulse to pull back from the tight-skinned face that was thrust so close to his own. He said nothing.

Dr. Zorak continued with a great show of friendliness. "In a few days the Station will be honored by a visit from an official government delegation," he said. "I should like to see you demonstrate this experiment, Stefan. So settle down and get it completed before they arrive and claim all my time."

Stefan looked up with interest. "I heard the lab technicians talking about some important visitors. Is that why they are all rushing around so busily?"

"We are all busy." As if reminded, Dr. Zorak straightened up and walked to the door. "I must go. See that you use your time well, boy."

Stefan nodded. "You can be sure of that. Thank you, Dr. Zorak, you have cleared up a number of problems for me."

As the lab door closed behind Dr. Zorak, Stefan grinned. "Thank you, oh, thank you again, Dr. Z. You don't know it, but you just told me how we can escape!"

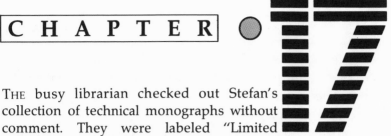

THE busy librarian checked out Stefan's collection of technical monographs without comment. They were labeled "Limited Circulation," but Stefan had carefully printed Dr. Zorak's name on the line following "Recommended by:".

He placed the bound booklets among his other papers and went directly to the lab. There he was greeted by a rustle of activity from the mouse cages.

"You fellows need some excitement in your lives," Stefan told them as he portioned out their food, "So I'm going to let you help me out with an experiment I'm about to do."

He set immediately to work. First he gathered the equipment he would need for his class work. He did just enough of the assignment to mislead a casually inquisitive eye. Then he opened the top drawer at the back of the table. Setting the monographs inside the drawer, he pulled up a stool and prepared to read. 'Now if someone comes in, I can close the drawer just by leaning forward,' he noted with satisfaction.

The first page of the monograph looked as if it were written in ancient Egyptian hieroglyphics. The next sheets, too, were filled with long equations and sprinkled with chemical symbols.

Stefan groaned. He remembered the triumphant note he'd planned to send to Evonn on his next run. He dug the folded paper out of his pocket.

> E.—*I've found a way! There's a drug that can lower body temperature. If we can get ours low enough, we can walk right through the Barriers without activating the laser beams. I'm making some today—Hooray!*
>
> S.

Stefan shook his head. 'I'll have to tone that note down a lot. This job is going to be harder than I thought.'

He held the paper over a hot spot on the tabletop. It disappeared in a whiff of smoke.

Again he turned to the monograph in the open drawer. After a careful reading, the maze of symbols began to make some sense. The second monograph was easier to understand, and he read through it rapidly.

The drug, Vitadorm, was compounded from three chemicals, two of which were common to any well-equiped lab. The third he had to synthesize himself.

By afternoon, Stefan had produced five vials of Vitadorm in varying strengths. He put them on a tray with five colored ink markers and carried them over to the mouse cages.

"This won't hurt much," he assured the first wriggling animal as he lifted it out of the cage. He injected it with the drug and painted a dot of orange on the underside of one paw. On the vial, he also marked an orange dot. The next mouse and vial were marked with a green dot; then he used yellow, red, and blue. At last five mice had all been injected with the drug in varying degrees of strength.

"Now just relax," Stefan told the mice. "Some of you may get cold and sleepy, but it won't last long. I'll be back to check your temperatures soon."

Stefan then cleaned away all signs of his secret work and picked up an armload of books. Before he left the lab, he stopped once more at the mouse cages. "Remember, if anyone comes in, keep your color spots hidden!" he said.

He jogged over to the main building. His timing was perfect—Marya was just walking down the front steps. As he ran past her, he whispered, "Bring my book to me!"

He let a volume slip out from under his arm and fall to the ground.

Marya was quick to grasp his intent. "Stefan," she called, "you dropped your book!" When he turned, she was already

hurrying towards him with the volume in her outstretched hand.

"Good idea, Stefan," she said quietly. "I do need to talk to you. If anyone is watching, this will look perfectly natural."

"Were you able to contact Professor Lev?" he asked as he reached for the book.

"Yes, I was. This is the best plan he could work out on such short notice. On Wednesday at 0300, you and Evonn are to be in the small grove of oak trees, ten kilometers east of Outguard Station Three of the Outer Barrier."

Stefan repeated the directions rapidly. "Then Evonn and I should try to go through the Barriers just below those trees so that we can use them as landmarks. Does a road go near there, Marya? How will we get away?"

"I only know that the grove will be easy for you to locate and that someone will be waiting there for you. If you fail to arrive by 0300, your contact will leave."

Stefan felt the panic inside him begin to rise again. He swallowed. "Thank you, Marya. I'll tell Evonn."

With a wave of his hand, he crossed the grass to his usual jogging route. At the second rest stop, he paused only long enough to write his note to Evonn and scale it across the grass. "We can't afford to make any mistakes," he had written, "from now on, every move counts."

The warm spring sunlight was beginning to wane as Stefan finished his run. It was time to make a temperature check on his mice. Anxiety raised a rash of gooseflesh on his arms as he approached the lab.

'Poor old Blue Spot is probably dreaming that he fell into the deep freeze by now,' he thought, 'but one of the others has just *got* to have had the right dose!'

Just as Stefan placed his finger on the thumbprint lock at the lab door, Professor Eisenberg came puffing up beside him.

"Stefan! At last I've caught up with you." A worried frown

furrowed his forehead. "I checked your work sheet earlier and saw that you had signed into the lab. But by time I got here, you were gone again."

Stefan's heart fell. What a time to be interrupted! He pushed the lab door aside and entered, with Professor Eisenberg close at his heels.

"I received a memo from Dr. Zorak this morning, Stefan." The Professor continued, "He won't be able to come to your demonstration, after all. Two members of the government delegation are arriving today, and he'll be busy now for the rest of the week."

"That's good news," said Stefan. "I mean, it will give me more time."

Professor Eisenberg rubbed his eyes wearily. "Not really, Stefan. Dr. Zorak wants you finished and cleared out of the lab by Wednesday afternoon."

Stefan looked up at him out of the corners of his eyes. "Do you get the idea that he's hurrying me out of sight?"

Professor Eisenberg seemed surprised at that question. "Oh, no, Stefan. Dr. Zorak is deeply concerned about you. In fact, he has instructed me to spend more time with you from now on. He seems to think that Professor Lev left you unsupervised too often."

Stefan winced. "I know that Zorak thinks I would have progressed faster if Professor Lev had worked with me more closely. Actually, I learn best when I have to figure things out for myself. I hate people watching me all the time!"

Professor Eisenberg nodded. "Well, let's go over the first three steps of the experiment together. Dr. Zorak made his wishes quite clear."

Stefan was trapped. He had so little time, and now he wouldn't be able to get near his mice to check their vital responses.

Professer Eisenberg looked up and caught one of Stefan's anxious glances in the direction of the mice cages.

"Have you been taking good care of those mice, Stefan? They seem awfully quiet today." He put down the beaker he was holding and started toward the mice.

"They are just fine, sir!" Stefan answered loudly. "I treat them like babies—the best of everything!"

Professor Eisenberg kept on walking.

"Professor...!" Stefan called, desperately trying to draw the man's attention away from the drugged mice. "Did—did you know that Dr. Zorak used to know my father years ago? Perhaps you've heard of him—Dr. Grigory Metvedenko."

This time Professor Eisenberg stopped dead in his tracks. He seemed to shrivel inside his white lab coat. When he turned, his face was gray.

"Metvedenko...your father? Surely you are mistaken!" His eyes flickered over Stefan's face. *"That's* who you... incredible!"

Stefan was horrified at what he was doing, but there was no way back now. "You must have known him, too, Professor! You are about the same age and in the same field of work!"

"No, no! I don't know who you are talking about. I had nothing to do with all that!"

The Professor darted a frantic look toward the patrol route outside the window. Then he leaped like a rabbit towards the door. Only when it stood open before him was he able to control himself.

"We will finish tomorrow, Stefan. Leave the lab immediately after you clean up!" He slid through the doorway and scurried away.

Stefan sank trembling onto the lab stool. 'He can't wait to get away from me,' he thought. 'I'm tainted with trouble, and he's scared stiff that he'll become involved.'

Feeling that events were closing in around him, Stefan gathered his sterile thermometers and hurried over to the mouse cages. Immediately his attention centered on the five little animals that were so critical to his escape plans.

As Stefan approached, Orange Spot crawled drunkenly to the door of his cage, begging for food. Green Spot gazed vacantly in his direction, his tiny body shuddering with cold. Yellow Spot had burrowed deep into his wood chip nest and would not respond.

A bolt of fear stiffened Stefan's spine as he bent over the last two cages. Both Red Spot and Blue Spot were dead!

# CHAPTER 18

THE road beside Stefan suddenly began to swarm with white mice. They came towards him, crawling in slow motion. One of the mice stopped and beckoned to him. Stefan saw that the mouse was Evonn. "Hurry, hurry!" said Evonn. Stefan tried to get up, but his legs wouldn't move. He called out "Help me!" and as he stretched out his hands, he saw that in the middle of his right palm there was a red spot!

Stefan sat up in his bed, his forehead beaded with a cold sweat. It was only a dream—or was it something more? A warning perhaps, an omen! He shook himself. There was no use trying to read meaning into dreams.

'I don't know which Red Spot I was supposed to be, anyway,' he thought. 'Since I made up that new batch of Vitadorm formula last night and injected a new bunch of mice, my dream could have about Red Spot #1 or Red Spot #2.'

The glowing numbers of his timepiece indicated that his alarm would go off in half an hour. 'I'll never get back to sleep now. I've just got to see how the mice made out on their new doses of the drug.'

He dressed hastily, checked out at the security desk, and ran to the lab. This time he went directly to Red Spot and Blue Spot. With shaking hands he opened their cages. Both mice were in a deep sleep, but breathing regularly.

Stefan checked the places in each cage where he had hidden morsels of cheese. Both mice had found and eaten them before falling asleep.

"Good," he whispered. "You must have been alert to figure out how to get those last two pieces. Now if you're still in good shape when you wake up, I'll feel much better."

In the meantime Stefan would make up the Vitadorm for himself and Evonn. This would be the tricky part—adjusting the proportions from mouse strength to human strength.

He gave all the mice fresh lettuce and went back to his test tube. Swiftly, Stefan repeated the procedure he had worked out the day before. Only after he had formulated two vials of the final mix of Vitadorm did he pause to glance at his timepiece. It had taken him longer than he had expected. He wrote a final set of instructions to Evonn and wrapped them with one of the vials in a roll of green paper. At last he was ready to deliver the package on his morning jog.

Every guard Stefan passed seemed to eye him suspiciously. Every locked door reminded him of how tightly the network of security was drawn about the Station. Only after the drug was safely across the Barrier was he able to breathe normally again.

Stefan timed his return to his own wing to coincide with the second caretaker's patrol. Marya was expecting him.

"I've hidden some dark clothes in your waste bag," she greeted him, getting straight to the point. "How is your experiment going?"

"The drug should go through another set of tests, but there isn't time. The problem is that our temperature must be as low as 37 degrees Celsius to prevent the lasers from activating. But if our temperature goes too low, we'll fall into a stupor." Stefan frowned. "I just hope Evonn will be able to follow my instructions. I wonder how he plans to get out of that building."

Marya shrugged. "He can take care of himself," she said. "Where are you going to meet him?"

"We decided that there will be no time to think of anything else until we're both outside those bloody Barriers, Marya. So we are going to meet just beyond the Outer Barrier, south of the grove of oak trees." Stefan took a deep breath and changed the subject. "I won't see you again, Marya. Thank you—I'll never forget you. Never!"

Stefan swung away from the desk and hurried down the hall, swallowing a huge lump in his throat. Behind him, he could hear Marya blowing her nose noisily.

Once inside his room, Stefan quickly unrolled the bundle of clothes. He found a wool hat, some dark slippers, and a brown one-piece fatigue suit.

Carefully, he placed his vial and supplies in with the clothes. As he was rolling them tightly together, his timepiece went off.

'Oh, no,' he groaned. 'I'll have to show up at the media center as usual or someone will be sure to notice.' He picked up his folder case and hurried from the room.

In a far corner of the carrel-lined room, Stefan set up his hologramic lesson on English verbs. Soon he was lost in his own thoughts and plans.

A pencil prodded him sharply in the back. Stefan whirled about to find Professor Eisenberg standing over him. He seemed to have recovered his composure after yesterday's shock.

"The security report shows that you were in the lab at 0530 this morning, Stefan," he said accusingly. "You were told that you could not work there alone anymore. That could get us both in trouble."

"I didn't really work there, Professor," said Stefan lamely, "I was just reviewing the charts. You see, I woke up early and began to worry about having to rush through that experiment. I decided that I'd better re-check my data before we go on to the next procedure."

"You should have waited for me to accompany you. Evidently, Dr. Zorak hasn't had time to change your security clearance yet, so I shall have to do that myself." Professor Eisenberg's tongue flickered nervously across dry lips. "Tomorrow we will devote the entire day to your experiment in order to be finished and cleared up before Dr. Zorak conducts his tour through the facilities."

"Oh yes," replied Stefan, "Dr. Zorak told me about his official visitors when he came to the lab the other day." Then with a flash of inspiration, he added: "He gave me some valuable insights into the modern uses of cryobiology."

Professor Eisenberg seemed surprised. "But he has never worked in the pure sciences."

"Perhaps not, Professor, but he was chief psychologist on a government project that involved the effects of low temperatures on the human body."

Professer Eisenberg took an involuntary step backwards.

"Th–that was a long time ago," he stammered, evidently remembering again the circumstances. "I must be going now, Stefan. I have official duties of my own to attend to."

He left Stefan wondering again whether he had acted wisely. The boy finally shrugged and snapped on the holograph. 'I might as well make things as confusing as possible around here. Who knows, Dr. Zorak may have a hard time explaining why he let me sign out that monograph on Vitadorm. And now Professor Eisenberg thinks that Zorak was in the lab with me teaching me all about cryobiology, too!'

This reverie was followed by another thought, and that one as unpleasant as the other one was pleasant.

'Oh, no! Now Professor Eisenberg will change my security clearance and I won't be able to get back into the lab! Now I'll never know if Red Spot woke up!'

# CHAPTER

STEFAN'S late afternoon jog was slow and purposeful. He took a last look at the lay of the land he would be covering that night in the dark. From the most westerly point on his route, he could just see Outguard Station Three, which he knew was beyond the Outer Barrier. Turning his eyes northward, he saw a straggling line of willows that marked the banks of a small stream. Following this for several kilometers, he finally located the stand of oaks. Everything was just as Marya had described it.

As he ran the return stretch on his route, Stefan tried to compare what he had just seen with the information he had sent to Evonn earlier. Fervently he hoped that his own directions had been as clear as those Professor Lev had given Marya for him.

That evening, after a shower and a light dinner, Stefan tried to rest while waiting out the remaining hours. He found that as the time for action drew closer, the fever pitch of excitement within him began to level off. It was now up to fate; he had done as much as he could.

At 0100, Stefan rose quietly and unrolled his bundle of supplies. His hand trembled as he removed the stopper to the vial of Vitadorm. Closing his eyes, Stefan probed the silence with his mind. He knew that somewhere in the building across the way Evonn, too, would be drinking the cloudy liquid.

"Evonn," he whispered, "here's to us—the beginning or the end."

The drug rolled down his throat, leaving a metallic taste in his mouth. 'Maybe it won't even work,' he thought. 'What if I wake up tomorrow morning and everything is just the same?'

He was sure that he would rather die.

At 0130, keys rattled softly in his door and the night caretaker poked his head inside. He took a routine look about and closed the door again.

Immediately, Stefan leaped to his feet and dressed in the dark clothes. He crept down the hall to the recycling chute built into the wall next to the storeroom. Climbing through the opening feet first, he managed to yank the door closed behind him as his body slipped downward in the smooth metal tube. After a breathtaking drop, he landed with a thud in a bin of soft goods. As Marya had explained, the bin stood next to a conveyor belt that transferred the material to the recycling unit in the next building. Stefan inched his way out the small square opening and fell headlong into the shadowy courtyard.

Here, Stefan paused a moment to check out his reactions to the drug. 'Hands and feet cold,' he noted methodically. 'Temperature dropping.' He pulled the dark hat low on his forehead. His timepiece showed 0145. He must move quickly now.

Stefan crept along the courtyard wall and slipped through a low hedge at the corner of the building. Heavy footsteps crunched towards him on the gravel path. With a pounding heart, he ducked behind the hedge. Again, Marya's information proved to be correct.

After the guard passed, Stefan struck out across the clipped grass towards his first goal—the Inner Barrier. Gradually he felt the sensation of cold creep throughout his body. His teeth began to chatter. Even the slight spring breezes that whispered against his cheeks made him shudder. 'My temperature is dropping fast now,' he thought. 'I've got to cover ground quickly before the chill gets into my muscles.'

Keeping his body low against the horizon, Stefan pressed onward at a steady pace. His fingers and toes ached with cold and soon his feet became so numb he felt as if he were running on wooden stumps. At last he found the faint path of flattened grass made by the recent Barrier Patrol. The Barrier itself then must be about a meter in front of his nose.

'This is it,' he thought, 'the final test of my homemade Vitadorm. Either I make it or I'll never know what hit me.' After a few false starts, he held his breath and lunged forward into the path of deadly crisscrossing lasers. He landed on the other side untouched.

"What do you know," he whispered, "I'm still alive!" Shivering, he wrapped his arms about himself. He was almost too cold to care.

Once more Stefan set out across seemingly endless meadows, now towards the Outer Barrier. To his dulled senses it seemed as if he had slipped inside his terrifying dream of the other night. He felt himself moving in slow motion. His stiff muscles could no longer answer the cry of his mind—hurry, hurry, hurry! Finally, Stefan's legs balked at carrying the weight of his body, and he dropped to his knees. Onward he crawled from bush to bush, tuft to tuft, blade to blade.

In the frozen silence, he gradually became aware of something damp and scratchy pressing against his face. He jerked his head back and found that he had fallen forward into the coarse grass. How long he had lain there he didn't know, but now his labored heartbeats seemed to jar the earth beneath him. As he sucked in the sweet night air in huge gulps, his memory began to return. 'Where am I?' he wondered. Far behind him, floodlit granite buildings squatted amongst the rolling foothills. Behind him still, but several kilometers to the west, was an Outguard Station. Nearby, Stefan saw the dark outline of some great trees towering against the moonlit sky.

"Trees...oak trees..." he whispered. "A stand of oaks..." He struggled to remember their significance, and then with a small cry, he rose to his knees.

'I've made it! I've made it!' he exulted. 'I'm on the outside at

last! I must have passed through the Outer Barrier without even knowing it.' His sense of relief was so great that he rolled sideways on the ground laughing weakly. As he moved, a painful prickling, like ten thousand needles, began to jab into Stefan's limbs. The blood was pulsing freely again through his limbs.

That meant something important! Stefan glanced at his timepiece. It was already 0255—just five minutes to 'meet' time. Where was Evonn? If his own dose of the drug was wearing off, Evonn's must be doing so, too. It might already be too late for him to get through the lasers!

Stefan stretched out tensely in the grass. Gathering every last shred of energy, he concentrated it into a mental message to his clone-brother.

'Come *now*, Evonn. I am waiting for you as we planned. You must hurry!'

There was nothing he could do but wait. He could not go back, and he would not go on without Evonn.

Until now, Stefan had never allowed himself to think beyond the actual moment of escape. But as he lay waiting on the other side of the Barriers, a jumble of questions rose to the surface of his mind.

'What will happen to Evonn and me now? Where will we be taken? Can we ever fit into a normal way of life? Will we be able to find out what happened to our clone-father, Metvedenko?'

And, almost against his will, Stefan recognized the most awful question of all. 'What will Dr. Zorak do when he discovers the double escape?' A nightmare of possibilities paraded through Stefan's imagination.

How had a man as intelligent as Dr. Zorak become so entangled in bitterness and revenge? Stefan puzzled. Now that he was free of the man, he could almost view him calmly.

'I guess Zorak is so crazy for power that he wants to control everything—even people's lives. If they don't cooperate, he finds ways to force them. And yet,' Stefan shook his head wonderingly, 'there's something pathetic about him. He really seems to want people to like him and think he's great. Maybe that's why he can't take it if anyone goes against him. He turns nasty fast. Poor Metvedenko found that out!'

Stefan rose into a crouch position and stared into the blank darkness behind him. Did he see something moving out there? Was it friend or foe? He waited, rooted to the spot. Powerful wings beat the air nearby and then the sharp cry of a field mouse splintered the silence. Stefan cringed, remembering that here, too, the game of prey and predator was played for keeps.

A vision of Dr. Zorak's angry face swam before Stefan's eyes, and a black tide of fear flooded his being. With it came a sudden flash of insight.

'Despite what I know about him now, Zorak *could* have won this game—could have won it long ago! If he had come to me when I was a little boy and all alone, I would have trusted him. I would have been his slave. Why didn't he do it? He's a psychologist and must know these things.'

Stefan struggled with that question, twisting it one way and another. There was only one answer that made sense.

'It must be that Zorak sort of outsmarted himself. He would have thought it safer to stay away from us as long as Metvedenko's sudden disappearance was fresh in people's minds. And then he would have waited until he was sure the cloning experiment would be successful in the long run—after all, Evonn and I might have developed into identical idiots! And then he probably wanted to be sure of his own official position before taking any risks with us.'

Little by little the events of the past were merging with the present.

'A few more years of intrigue,' Stefan mused, 'and Zorak would be in a position secure enought to cover up all his private deals. But Evonn and I found each other too soon!'

This brought Stefan back to the present, and he glanced anxiously at his timepiece. Two more minutes had passed! Professor Lev's warning had been clear... if the boys were not at the meet place by 0300, their contacts would have to leave without them.

'Should I go?' Stefan could no longer avoid the question. 'Should I go alone... can I ever go on alone again?' Perhaps he had already developed the 'clone mentality' that Professor Lev had warned him about!